"Wow! Kara Lennox's BLOND JUSTICE series has it all—smart, determined heroines, ya-gotta-love-'em macho heroes, taut suspense and romance that will steam your glasses while it melts your heart. Each book is a winner; together they're pure magic."
                    —Bestselling author Merline Lovelace

Dear Reader,

I often write about heroines who are slightly offbeat, but Brenna Thompson, my debutante-in-denial, takes the cake. Perhaps that's because she's a lot like me—petite, unconventional, creative. I even gave her my hair (which is currently in blond spikes), my former downtown loft and my love for silver charms. (Unlike Brenna, however, I'm not an heiress, darn it.)

Who better to match up with Brenna than uptight FBI special agent Heath Packer, who would never dream of breaking the rules. Or would he? I'll just tell you that Heath isn't all he first appears to be.

I hope you have fun with Brenna and Heath as they continue the search for con man Marvin Carter, which began in *Hometown Honey* (HAR #1068). This story will take you on a wild romp from Cottonwood, Texas, to New Orleans, Dallas and finally New York. I don't want to give too much away, but vengeance is sweet, and it involves an ice sculpture and an empty elevator shaft.

All my best,

Kara Lennox

Downtown DEBUTANTE

KARA LENNOX

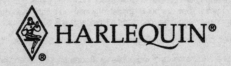

HARLEQUIN®

TORONTO • NEW YORK • LONDON
AMSTERDAM • PARIS • SYDNEY • HAMBURG
STOCKHOLM • ATHENS • TOKYO • MILAN • MADRID
PRAGUE • WARSAW • BUDAPEST • AUCKLAND

ISBN 0-373-75085-4

DOWNTOWN DEBUTANTE

Copyright © 2005 by Karen Leabo.

This edition published by arrangement with Harlequin Books S.A.

® and TM are trademarks of the publisher. Trademarks indicated with ® are registered in the United States Patent and Trademark Office, the Canadian Trade Marks Office and in other countries.

www.eHarlequin.com

Printed in U.S.A.

ABOUT THE AUTHOR

Texas native Kara Lennox has been an art director, typesetter, textbook editor and reporter. She's worked in a boutique, a health club and an ad agency. She's been an antiques dealer and even a blackjack dealer. But no work has made her happier than writing romance novels.

When not writing, Kara indulges in an ever-changing array of weird hobbies. (Her latest passions are treasure hunting and creating mosaics.) She loves to hear from readers. You can visit her Web page and drop her a note at www.karalennox.com.

Books by Kara Lennox

HARLEQUIN AMERICAN ROMANCE

Don't miss any of our special offers. Write to us at the following address for information on our newest releases.

Harlequin Reader Service
U.S.: 3010 Walden Ave., P.O. Box 1325, Buffalo, NY 14269
Canadian: P.O. Box 609, Fort Erie, Ont. L2A 5X3

My gratitude to FBI Special Agent
Jennifer Coffindaffer for her help with researching
FBI procedures. Any mistakes are mine.

Prologue

Brenna Thompson drew herself deeper into the down comforter, trying to reclaim the blessed relief of sleep. But instead of drifting back down, she awoke with a jolt and smacked into hard reality. She was stranded in Cottonwood, Texas, without a dime to her name, her entire future hanging by a thread.

And someone was banging on her door at the Kountry Kozy Bed & Breakfast.

Wearing only a teddy, she slid out of bed and stumbled to the door. "I told you to take the key," she said grumpily, opening the door, expecting to see Cindy, her new roommate. "What time is it, any—" She stopped as her bleary eyes struggled to focus. Standing in the hallway was a broad-shouldered man in a dark suit, a blindingly white shirt and a shimmering blue silk tie. He was at least a foot taller than Brenna's own five foot three, and she had to strain her neck to meet his cool, blue-eyed gaze. Another man stood behind the first, but he was in shadow—like he was trying to be in the background.

In a purely instinctual gesture, she slammed the door in his face. My God, she was almost naked. A stranger in a suit had seen her almost naked. Her whole body flushed, then broke out in goose bumps.

The knock came again, softer this time, but firm.

"Uh, just a minute!" She didn't have a robe. She wasn't a robe-wearing sort of person. But she spied a robe belonging to Sonya, her other roommate, lying at the foot of her bed. The white silk garment trailed the floor, the sleeves hanging almost to Brenna's fingertips—Sonya was tall—but at least it sort of covered her.

Taking a deep breath, she opened the door again. "Yes?"

Still there. Still just as tall, just as imposing, just as—handsome. Not her type, she thought quickly. But there was a certain commanding presence about this stranger that made her stomach swoop and her palms itch.

"Brenna Thompson?"

Deep voice. It made all her hair follicles stand at attention.

"Yes, that's me." He didn't smile, and a frisson of alarm wiggled through her body. "Is something wrong? Oh, my God, did something happen to someone in my family?"

He hesitated fractionally. "No. I'm Special Agent Heath Packer with the FBI. This is Special Agent Pete LaJolla."

The other man stepped closer and nodded a greeting. They both looked as if they expected to enter.

Brenna glanced over her shoulder. The room was a complete wreck. Every available surface was covered with clothes and girlie stuff, not to mention baby things belonging to Cindy's little boy. Even fastidious Sonya's bed was unmade. Sonya was used to servants doing that sort of thing for her.

Special Agent No. 1 didn't wait for her consent. He eased past her into the room, his observant gaze taking everything in.

"If you'd given me some warning, I could have tidied up," she groused, pulling the robe more tightly around her. She hadn't realized how thin the fabric was.

Mustering her manners, Brenna cleared off a cosmetics case and a pair of shoes from the room's only chair. "Here, sit down. You're making me nervous. And…Agent LaJolla, was it?" She brushed some clothes off Sonya's twin bed. La Jolla nodded and sat gingerly on the bed while Brenna retreated to her own bed. She sat cross-legged on it, drawing the covers over her legs both for warmth and modesty.

"I assume you know why we're here," Packer said, easing his tall frame into the wingback chair. He looked even more masculine, surrounded by chintz and lace and cabbage roses.

"Something to do with Marvin Carter, I would guess. Does this mean someone is finally taking our case seriously? That other FBI guy in Louisiana—Del Roy or whatever his name was—he could hardly be bothered." Indignation welled up in Brenna's chest. "Big deal, three dumb blondes lost their life savings. Like, who cares? But I guess that suitcase full of cash caught your attention." Brenna, Cindy and Sonya, all of them victims of the same con man, had tracked him to Louisiana and flushed him out, with no help from the FBI. As a result, they recovered Cindy's money—$300,000 in cash—though Marvin himself got away.

While LaJolla studied his fingernails in a bored manner, Packer studied Brenna, and she could almost see the gears turning behind his eyes, carefully calculating his answer. "We'd like to hear the facts of the case from you firsthand. And, if you don't mind…" He pulled a microcassette recorder from his jacket pocket and set it on the tiny table next to the chair. He also brought out a notebook and pen.

"No, I don't mind." After he made a few preliminary comments for the tape—date, time, location and who was present—she told him her story, from beginning to end. She started with how the famous art agent "Seneca Dealy" had found her at a neighborhood art fair and had promised to pluck her from obscurity and make her a jeweler to the stars. "He said everything I wanted to hear," Brenna said. "Starving artists thrive on praise and high hopes, you know."

"And did you also have a sexual relationship with this Seneca?"

"I'm sure you know I did," she said testily, her face burning. She wasn't some virginal prude, easily embarrassed, but neither was she eager to dwell on her stupidity where Marvin was concerned. "I don't see how the details of *that* could be any use to you."

"His behavior is very important," Packer countered. "I need to know the exact details of how this guy operates."

"Fine." She took a deep breath and gave the agent what he'd asked for—exact details. "He's very good in bed. He always wears a condom. He prefers Trojans. Is that what you want to know?"

LaJolla was trying not to laugh, but Packer dutifully took down every word. "Interesting to know about the condoms. He takes risks in some areas, not in others. Go on."

She sighed, her anger evaporating. "He wasn't all bad," she admitted. "As an artist, sometimes I lack confidence in my abilities. He boosted my self-esteem. Because of him, I got the courage to submit my designs to a committee that runs the IJC show. You know what that is?"

"I'm not familiar with IJC."

"International Jewelry Consortium. They run the most exclusive jewelry and gem show in the country. Only a select few dealers and designers are invited to exhibit. And they chose me." She still felt pride glowing inside her every time she thought about that phone call where they'd told her she was in the show. It was the career break she'd been working toward for five years.

"Congratulations," Packer said politely, though she knew he had no idea what a big deal it was.

"I worked like crazy to get some very special pieces ready for the show," she continued. "I had some fabulous stones left to me by my grandmother. Anyway, I woke up one morning and everything was gone. Everything. My checking account was empty and so was my trust fund."

"How did he get to a trust fund?" LaJolla said, speaking up for the first time. "Don't those have pretty strict security?"

"Well, it wasn't a real trust fund. I just called it that. It was an account my father put money into every month for my support, because he thought I couldn't take care of myself. But I never touched it." She'd planned to donate it to charity someday. *See, Dad? I didn't need your old money after all.*

"But you did accept the money," said Packer.

"Why do you care about that, anyway? It's gone, that's what matters."

"Just trying to get a complete picture," he said mildly.

She told him the rest of the story—how Sonya, a debutante from Houston, had tracked her down after Marvin wiped her out, and how the two of them had followed a trail of clues to Cottonwood, where they found Cindy. The three spurned and destitute women—The Blondes, or The Blond Posse, as some people in Cottonwood affectionately called them—had pledged to bring Marvin to justice. The last time they'd seen him, he'd been running naked down the main street of a small Louisiana town—humiliated, but free.

When the story wound down, Packer shut off the recorder and packed up as if ready to leave. "So what are you going to do?" Brenna asked.

"We have to check out a few things," Agent Packer said noncommittally. "We'll be back in touch." A look passed between the two agents.

Brenna was pretty sure she knew what it meant. *We'll be back in touch—when hell freezes over.* "So I'll never hear from you again. No one was murdered, no one was kidnapped. Why would the FBI waste its time?"

"Ms. Thompson, I assure you," Packer said. "You haven't seen the last of me."

As he walked out of the room without a backward glance, Brenna pondered his parting shot. Had it been a promise…or a threat?

HEATH PACKER CLIMBED behind the wheel of his dark blue Chrysler LeBaron while Pete LaJolla, a bit out of breath from the short walk, slid into the passenger seat.

"You gonna tell me what that was about? I thought we were going to arrest her."

Heath started the engine. He made one circuit around Cottonwood's town square, marveling at the quaintness of it all as he processed what he'd just learned about Brenna Thompson. "She doesn't know she's a suspect."

"Yeah, so?"

LaJolla was an okay guy, but not the brightest bulb in the marquee. "She thinks she got away with her crime. She thinks her parents would be too embarrassed to turn her in."

"So…if she thinks she's gotten away with her crime… she'll get careless?"

Packer nodded. "And she'll lead us to the Picasso."

"You think this Marvin person has the painting? Who the hell is Marvin Carter, anyway? And what's all this about a suitcase full of money?"

"Guess we better find out."

Brenna Thompson had been a surprise in more ways than one. It wasn't just her attire, or lack of it, that had thrown Heath off balance. He smiled now as he thought about how she'd looked when she'd opened the door, fuzzy from sleep, her platinum-frosted hair sticking out at odd angles from her head, mascara rings under her eyes. And that body. Small as she was, she had enough curves to inspire a roller-coaster designer. And in that tiny slip of silk she'd been wearing, he'd gotten an eyeful.

But even fully clothed—well, if you could call wearing a transparent robe fully clothed—there'd been a certain quality about her that surprised the hell out of him.

She was cute. Okay, cute and sexy as hell. And what a mouth. Not just the pink, pouty lips, but what had come through them. She seemed as open and honest and unpretentious as a daisy. Certainly not like any fugitive felon he'd ever seen.

"She was kind of hot, huh?" LaJolla commented. Then he watched Heath carefully for a reaction.

Damn. This was an important case. The Thompsons were influential people. If he solved it, if he recovered the stolen painting, maybe he could put the past behind him. Focusing on Brenna Thompson's sexy mouth wasn't the place to start.

Heath turned into the alley behind the empty office they'd been using as a surveillance base. "I don't think she's anything special."

Chapter One

It was November, and Heath Packer was sweating. It was only about seventy degrees, a temperature that would have been heaven in any other part of the country. But here in New Orleans, the air was still and the humidity hovering at a hundred percent. Plus, Heath was trapped in a car. Not even the tinted windows totally protected him from the sun's warming rays.

He'd been surprised when Brenna and Sonya had taken off in the middle of the night. He and LaJolla had gamely followed them all the way to southern Louisiana, where the two women had checked into the humble Magnolia Guest House. He could only assume this trip had something to do with Marvin Carter.

Heath's research into the Marvin Carter case had yielded lots of fascinating information about Brenna. Since no one else at the Bureau was much interested in Carter—as Brenna had indicated—Heath had taken over the case and combined it with the Thompson case. All indications were that Marvin Carter and Brenna Thompson were partners, while Sonya Patterson and Cindy Lefler Rheems were mere patsies. However, Heath had yet to put all the pieces of the puzzle together.

"You haven't done much surveillance in a warm climate," observed Grif Hodges, an agent out of New Orleans who'd been brought in on the case, since it was now in their backyard. Mercifully, the humorless LaJolla had gone back to Dallas.

Grif, a New Orleans native, had on gym shorts and a T-shirt. Heath was stuck in his regulation dress shirt and suit pants, his jacket and tie ready in case he had to do anything official.

They'd been parked on this street for an hour, watching Brenna's room.

Finally, just as Heath was forced to crack the windows or suffocate, the women emerged. Sonya, as always, was dressed to the nines in a silk blouse, a coordinating jacket, slim black pants and spike heels. But it was Brenna who drew his eye. She wore overalls with a pink tank top underneath. Yet even in such shapeless clothing, there was no disguising her full breasts or rounded bottom. As she locked the door, she laughed at something Sonya said.

Heath's mouth went dry. Who could believe such a perky pixie of a woman could have pulled off a world-class heist? But the evidence couldn't be more clear.

As the two women headed off on foot toward the French Quarter, Brenna's gaze swept the street. Heath's heart almost stopped beating when her eyes fixed on his car, and for a moment he was sure she'd spotted him. But then she looked away and they continued down the sidewalk.

The agents prepared to follow Sonya and Brenna on foot, but the women turned into a tiny café at the end of the block.

"I'll keep an eye on them," Grif offered. "You see if you can get into their room."

Adrenaline pumping, Heath quickly located the Magnolia's manager. The blue-haired lady who ran the guest house took one look at his credentials and had no problem letting him into Brenna's room.

"I'll let myself out and lock the door when I'm done," Heath said in a no-nonsense tone when Madame Blue Hair lingered in the doorway, looking worried.

"What do I tell them if they complain that someone was in their room?" she asked.

"They will never know I was here," Heath assured her, shooing her out the door. "And I know you won't tell them, will you?"

The room was small and spartan, with twin beds, a small table and chairs, a battered oak dresser and a noisy window air-conditioning unit. It looked as if each of the women had claimed a bed. The one by the far wall had only one open suitcase on it, a fancy brocade one, partially unpacked. Two matching suitcases were stacked in a corner.

The second bed was covered with wadded-up clothes. A plain black suitcase, also open, overflowed with what looked to be garments selected and rejected. Heath noticed the cream-colored silky tab of fabric peeking out. He couldn't resist pulling it out, recognizing it as the garment Brenna had been wearing when he'd first confronted her. It was so delicate that he could ball it up and make it disappear inside his fist.

He put it back where he'd found it. He wasn't here to entertain fantasies. He went through Brenna's suitcase first, finding nothing but clothing, shoes and toiletries. Next he checked the dresser drawers. The ones on Sonya's side were filled with neatly folded clothes. Brenna's were empty. Likewise the closet featured several color-coordinated outfits, dainty sweater sets and tailored pants with designer labels. No clothes that could possibly belong to Brenna.

He checked the bathroom. One set of cosmetics lined up precisely, all the same brand, all looking as if they had just been pulled from the department store display case. On the other side of the sink, mismatched drugstore make-up and toiletries spilled from three different zipper cases.

He checked everywhere. Nothing incriminating. No phone numbers or addresses or mysterious business cards that might explain Brenna's presence in New Orleans. Definitely no stolen oil paintings.

He went back to Brenna's suitcase and felt all around the inside. A suspicious thickness caught his attention. He realized there was a hidden zipper that had escaped his notice during the first inspection. He unzipped the secret compartment and reached inside.

Holy cow. Cash, enough to choke a rhinoceros. Now, this was interesting. Brenna had told him that Marvin Carter had stripped her clean, that she was destitute. He quickly counted it. Close to twelve thousand dollars.

He heard footsteps just outside and hastily returned the cash to its hiding place. When someone fitted a key into the door, he did the only thing he could think of—he darted into the closet. This search wasn't precisely illegal, because the manager had let him in. But it wasn't a hundred percent defensible, either. Besides, he didn't want to tip his hand yet. If Brenna knew she was under surveillance, she would never lead him to Marvin Carter and the stolen painting.

The door opened, and he expected to hear the women's voices. Instead he heard a man say a curt, "Thanks," and the door closed again. What the hell?

Heath opened the closet door a crack. A wide-shouldered man in a leather jacket had his back to Heath. He was looking around the room, not touching anything.

Could Heath possibly be this lucky? Had Marvin Carter just dropped into his lap? If he could capture both him and Brenna, surely one of them would flip on the other.

But when the man turned, Heath could see he looked nothing like the photos he'd seen of Marvin. This guy had shaggy blond hair, a square chin and chiseled cheekbones, nothing like Marvin's soft features and trim, dark hair.

Unlike Heath, the newcomer spent little time on Brenna's things, focusing instead on Sonya's suitcase. He methodically checked the contents, then put everything back just as he found it.

A noise at the door startled the intruder, and he froze. Another key scraped in the lock. This place was Grand Central Station.

Suddenly the blond man wrenched open the closet door and lunged inside, closing the door just as Brenna and Sonya entered.

"I can't believe you forgot the money," Sonya was saying. "How embarrassing."

"I got used to you paying for everything with your Visa," said Brenna. "At least they didn't make us wash dishes."

"Yeah, well, we better return pretty quick with some cash. I didn't like the way that waiter was looking at us."

Right about then, the blond man realized he was not alone in the closet. But he displayed unbelievable control, because he didn't make any noise except for a slightly audible intake of breath.

"Who the hell are you?" Heath whispered, pretty sure the women couldn't hear him over the drone of the air conditioner.

"I was about to ask the same thing," the blond man said.

"Wait," said Sonya. "I'm going to hang this jacket up. I don't need it." And she swung open the closet door.

She opened her mouth to scream, but she stopped herself as her shocked gaze locked on the other man. "John-Michael McPhee, what are you doing in my closet?"

Brenna joined her at the closet door, equally surprised. "Agent Packer?"

Heath was going to have to do some fast talking to get himself out of this one. He exchanged a glance with the other man as they both stepped out of the closet. And for one brief moment, he felt they were in sync. Neither of them was supposed to be here, and they'd both been caught. And unless Heath missed his guess, McPhee had some law enforcement training.

He sensed an ally.

And speaking of allies, where was Grif? If he'd been keeping his eye on the women, he would know by now Heath was caught in here. Then he saw a face at the window. Grif caught his eye, smiled and waved, then disappeared. Apparently Grif had read the situation accurately, saw there was no immediate danger and had decided not to interfere.

"Your mother sent me to find you, Sonya," McPhee began. "You're supposed to be at Elizabeth Arden."

Sonya sank onto her bed and folded her arms. "I'm not a child. I can come and go as I please."

"Not when your mom's footing the bill, you can't. She got the Visa statement. There were charges from all over Texas and Louisiana. She was afraid you'd been kidnapped."

"That does not explain why you broke into my hotel room."

Brenna pointed at Heath. "And it doesn't explain what

he's doing here." She fastened her icy blue eyes on him. "I bet you're not even FBI."

Heath quickly produced his Bureau identification, which Brenna inspected thoroughly, as if she would know real credentials from fake ones. "I saw this guy coming into your room," he improvised. "At first I thought he was your runaway fiancé. I came in thinking I would make an arrest."

He glanced over at the other man, who amazingly did not contradict him.

"So you've been following me," Brenna said on a rising note.

Heath saw no way out of this. "Yes, I was following you. I thought you might be protecting your fiancé. It's a perfectly natural assumption. Romeo con men often inspire loyalty in their victims."

"So you feel you were perfectly justified entering our room without our permission," Brenna said, looking at first one man, then the other. "We could have *you* arrested," she said, jabbing her finger into McPhee's chest. Then she turned back to Heath. She almost jabbed him, too, then stopped at the last minute, as if she'd thought better of it. "And you. Unless you have a search warrant, I could have your badge."

The last thing Heath needed was someone trying to get him fired. After his troubles in Baltimore, he was already skating on thin ice. Supervisory Special Agent Fleming Ketcher would have kittens if he knew Heath had been caught in an iffy search.

McPhee, obviously not intimidated by Brenna's bravado, ignored her and sat on the bed next to Sonya. "I was worried about you, that's all," he said, his voice soft. "I really did believe someone might have kidnapped you."

Sonya was unaffected by his attempt to mollify. "The

only person you care about is yourself. If anything happened to me, you'd look pretty bad."

"Sonya, you know that's not true. Tell me what's going on."

She considered her reply for several long seconds. "Brenna's an old friend, a sorority sister." Brenna's eyebrows flew up, but she said nothing. "Pretty soon I'm going to be an old stodgy married woman," Sonya continued. "Mother had the wedding under control. I just wanted to have some fun, get it out of my system."

Sonya was lying through her teeth. It sounded like she hadn't admitted to anyone she'd been snookered by a con man. In fact, it appeared as if this John-Michael McPhee— a family friend?—and Sonya's mother believed she was still engaged to Marvin.

Heath wasn't going to rain on her parade. That was for her to sort out with her family. His concern was Brenna, the depth of whose involvement in Marvin's various schemes was yet to be determined.

McPhee seemed to be evaluating Sonya's explanation. But it was hard to tell whether he believed her or not. Finally he said, "Sonya, you need to come home. Your mother's not well."

Sonya rolled her eyes. "Mother's never well. She's the biggest hypochondriac I've ever known."

"She's not kidding around this time. She's in the hospital. She's...she's had a heart attack."

Brenna's hand went to her mouth in alarm, while Sonya went white as a marble statue. "Oh, my God," she murmured. "Is she okay? John-Michael, tell me the truth."

"She's stable. But you need to come home. Now."

She nodded. "I'll get packed. Would you wait for me outside, please? I'll only be a minute."

McPhee hesitated, then nodded. He stood, gave Heath a skeptical look, then held out his hand. "John-Michael McPhee. Thanks for not shooting me."

Heath took the proffered hand. "Heath Packer. I usually ask questions first, then shoot."

As Sonya threw clothes into her suitcase, McPhee headed for the exit. Brenna opened the door for him, giving him an unmistakable warning look. Then she transferred her attention to Heath. "You, too."

"I need to talk—"

"Get a warrant."

"Oooookay." At least she wasn't on the phone to his boss. Yet. Fleming Ketcher would not find this situation amusing.

ONCE THE INTERLOPING MEN were safely outside and the door closed, Brenna turned to Sonya. "Who *is* that gorgeous guy?"

Sonya continued packing without looking at Brenna, her movements sharp and ultraefficient. "He's my bodyguard."

Brenna couldn't help it. She laughed. "You have a bodyguard?"

"It's my mother's idea. I've told you she's a bit overprotective. After what happened to my father, can you blame her?"

Brenna sobered at the reminder. "So your mother doesn't know about Marvin being a con man?"

"I couldn't bring myself to tell her. All this time she thought I was chilling out at a spa. I didn't think she'd worry. I mean, she *never* looks at her Visa bill. She has a financial manager who pays her bills."

"You'll have to tell her now."

"I suppose." Sonya looked up, her eyes filling with tears. "Oh, Brenna, she was so happy. Planning this wedding was the high point of her life. Since I became engaged, she's talked of nothing but creating the perfect ceremony for the perfect princess bride. I couldn't take that away from her."

As flawed as Sonya's logic was, Brenna understood. After all, she hadn't told her own parents that her wealthy, suave art-agent fiancé was a big phony. It was a very tough thing, admitting not just that you were a fool, but a destitute one. But at least Brenna's family hadn't gotten to the wedding-plan stage.

"I'm sorry to leave you like this," Sonya said. "I think you should give up the hunt for now. It's not safe, and Marvin could be dangerous. Or…you could hook up with the FBI agent."

Brenna snorted. "Yeah, right. He thinks I'm protecting Marvin. Of all the stupid assumptions."

"He had to make sure," Sonya said. "He was probably going by the statistics. After all, it would be easy for a naive woman to convince herself there'd been some mistake, that the love of her life hadn't really stolen from her, that the FBI was in error. Agent Packer has no way of knowing you aren't one of those women."

"I can't believe you're defending him. He sneaked into our room! He was probably looking through our underwear."

Sonya's face hardened. "John-Michael is the one who broke in. Agent Packer was just trying to protect us."

Brenna supposed that was marginally true, at least if she could believe Packer's story.

"Promise me you won't try to catch Marvin on your own," Sonya said. "I don't want to have to worry about you."

Under the circumstances, Brenna had no choice. "I promise. Don't give me another thought. You just go home and take care of your mother."

Sonya zipped up her last suitcase. "I feel so guilty, making her worry." She bit her lip. "I probably caused her heart attack."

"You didn't know she was ill. Don't do this to yourself, Sonya." Brenna went to Sonya and hugged her. Other than coming from wealthy families, the two women didn't have a lot in common. They never would have sought each other out as friends under ordinary circumstances. But over the past few weeks, they'd shared a lot.

"With Cindy on her honeymoon and me going home," Sonya said, "I guess The Blond Posse is officially disbanded."

"I have a feeling we'll see each other again." Brenna helped Sonya carry her suitcases out. The bodyguard loaded them all in the trunk of his rental SUV as if they weighed nothing. Packer was nowhere to be seen, the traitor.

At the last minute Brenna took Sonya aside. "How well do you know this guy?"

"Way better than I ever wanted to. We grew up together, though he's a few years older than me. But Mother hired him as my bodyguard when I was eighteen."

"I could think of worse fates." The bodyguard wasn't hard to look at, but it was Heath Packer who'd caused Brenna's hormones to jump up and take notice.

"Ugh. Please." Sonya gave a very un-Sonya-like sneer. Then she gave Brenna a quick parting hug, climbed into the bodyguard's SUV and was whisked away.

Brenna felt a wave of loneliness. What was she going to do now? Sit back and let the FBI go after Marvin? Yeah, like they'd been so effective up until now. That jerk Packer was wasting his time suspecting *her,* instead of going after the real criminal.

She supposed she better pay her restaurant check before Willie-the-Cajun-Waiter-from-Hell came after her with his coffee pot.

She returned to her room, pulled a twenty from her stash—at least neither of the room-breakers had found her money—and headed back to the restaurant.

"Hey, Willie," she called to their surly waiter. "I got the cash." She waved her twenty at him. "I told you I was good for it."

Now Willie was all smiles. "Oh, not to worry, miss. Your bill was paid in full."

"Oh." Had Sonya—no, the SUV had driven down the street in the opposite direction. Then, somehow, without even seeing him, Brenna knew. She felt a tickle at the back of her neck and turned to see Heath Packer in a booth, eating a bowl of gumbo.

She marched over to the booth and slid in across from him. "So, you're still here. I suppose you expect me to slobber in gratitude for paying our bill."

He looked up from his gumbo. "A simple thanks would do."

She slapped her twenty on the table. "Here. I refuse to be beholden to you."

"Now there's no need—"

"How dare you think I'm so stupid that I would protect a guy who totally humiliated me and wiped me out, not to mention the damage he's done to my reputation? If I don't show up at that IJC show with my jewelry, my career is over!"

"I have to go with the information I have," Heath said

in an infuriatingly reasonable tone. "Agent Delacroix told me what happened in Faring, Louisiana. Your warning allowed Marvin Carter to escape."

"That was an accident. He wasn't supposed to see Cindy peeking in his window. Oh, why am I trying to explain anything to you?" Brenna stole a package of saltines from Heath and opened it.

"Didn't you just have lunch?" he asked.

"I have a fast metabolism."

Heath focused on his gumbo for a few minutes. He ate his way around the okra, she noticed. Obviously not a Southern boy.

"So what brought you to New Orleans?" he finally asked after a long, awkward silence.

"Internet sleuthing." Brenna's pride over how clever she and Sonya had been warred with her desire not to talk to Packer. Pride won out. "Sonya's first contact with Marvin was in a chat room, so we figured he might use that MO again. Sure enough, we spotted him in a singles chat room. Different name, but using the same tired lines. He was flirting with a woman called 'FrenchQuarterChic.' Before we could learn more, they both dropped off. I discovered he'd downloaded maps of New Orleans from my computer."

Packer gave Brenna a nod. "Good work."

"She's here, all right. And so is he."

"It's a pretty big city."

"I know. But I figure he might try to fence some of the stolen jewelry here. There are a ton of estate jewelers on Royal Street. I looked in the Yellow Pages."

HEATH HAD TO HAND IT to Brenna. She had a sharp mind. That was a pretty good story she'd cooked up—improbable, but barely believable. She also had quite an appetite. She polished off the last saltine from the cellophane packet, then started eyeing his cornbread muffin.

He pulled a paper napkin from the dispenser and set the muffin on it, pushing it toward her. "Jeez. I'd hate to see you if you missed a meal."

She dug into the muffin without so much as a thanks.

"So what are your plans?" Heath asked casually.

"I don't have any. I promised Sonya I wouldn't track down Marvin Carter on my own. She thinks it might be dangerous, and she doesn't want to worry about me."

"And I'm sure you wouldn't want to worry your old sorority sister."

Brenna surprised him by laughing. "That was pretty funny. Me, in a sorority. I wonder if Mr. Beefcake Bodyguard bought it?"

"You thought he was good-looking?"

She gave him a sideways look. "Oh, yeah."

And just what the hell had prompted him to ask a stupid question like that? Heath reminded himself to stick to business. Whom Ms. Brenna Thompson found attractive or unattractive was not his concern.

"Why does Sonya need a bodyguard?" he asked.

"She doesn't. But her mom's overprotective because Sonya's father was murdered when she was ten. Sonya's all her mother has left."

A nasty thought occurred to Heath. Had Brenna befriended Sonya to get close to the wealthy Mrs. Patterson? Looking at her now, nibbling at his muffin, he found it hard to suspect her. But that was his job, after all.

"Tell you what," he said. "Why don't the two of us work together?" This was the plan he and Grif had hastily come up with, now that she was on to their surveillance.

Heath would pretend to be her teammate. Since she didn't know Grif existed, he would continue to observe from a discreet distance to see if Brenna made contact with anyone when she thought no one was looking. Even now, Grif was seated at the opposite end of the restaurant, nursing a cup of coffee and reading a newspaper.

Heath hoped Brenna would make her move soon. Fleming Ketcher was pushing him to make the arrest, and was only marginally convinced that Heath's plan to give her some line was a better idea.

"I don't want to work with you," Brenna said. "I don't like you. You're sneaky, and you think I'm a liar, or stupid, or both."

"I don't think you're any of those things." It was partly the truth. He didn't think she was stupid. "I'm prepared to believe you really don't know where Marvin is, and that you're not protecting him."

"Well, gee, thanks."

He needed to convince her they were on the same side. "Listen, Brenna. Even if you don't like me, I have resources you don't. I have access to databases and a crime lab. And I can offer you some measure of protection."

"But why do you need me?" she asked, not unreasonably.

"You can identify both the stolen jewelry *and* Marvin. All I have are the rough drawings you provided, and a couple of blurry photographs of the perp."

He could see she was mulling over his words. On second thought, she was mulling over his gumbo. "Do you want something else to eat?"

She waved at Willie the waiter. "Can I have a bowl of that gumbo, please? Large."

Chapter Two

If this was what FBI agents did all day, Brenna thought, she wondered why she hadn't applied to the Bureau. She and Heath had spent all afternoon hitting every jewelry store in the French Quarter, checking out the inventory for any sign of Brenna's stolen pieces, then showing Marvin's photo to the proprietors asking if anyone had seen him.

No one had.

Still, Brenna was in her element. She lingered over some of the gaudy estate pieces, trying on rings that cost more than she made in a year, imagining how she might reinterpret the designs in her own style.

She also enjoyed watching Heath in his macho FBI role. The suit, the badge, the subtle bulge of his gun in its shoulder holster had seemed a bit out of place in Cotton-wood, Texas. But here in New Orleans, the costume afforded him respect. People took him seriously. They listened when he spoke. Some were decidedly afraid of him. And the women, especially, responded to him in an obviously sexual way, even the senior citizens.

She sighed. Respect was one thing she'd never really gotten in her life. As the youngest of six kids, she was the one always craning her neck, looking up to her big brothers and sisters.

Marvin had sensed that lack in her life. He'd known exactly what to say, how to look at her, how to listen to her, to make her believe he valued her as a person and recognized her intelligence and talent.

Intelligence. Right. She'd been a real smart one, letting a weasel into the chicken house.

"Brenna, let's go," Heath said impatiently. "We have a lot more shops to check in the French Quarter alone."

Brenna realized she'd been lost in thought as she gazed at an aquamarine brooch in the shape of a dragonfly. She could do dragonflies, she realized, sleek, modern critters that would look as if they'd lit for an instant on a scarf or jacket lapel, shimmering with pavé diamonds.

She shook her head to clear it. "Sorry. Can we stop and get something to eat?"

"Two lunches weren't enough?"

"It's almost four o'clock. Teatime. Come on, I'll treat," she said as they cut through the colorfully named Pirate's Alley to Jackson Square, where the living mosaic of sidewalk artists, musicians and mimes took Brenna's breath away.

Heath seemed not to notice any of it. Not even a child doing an energetic soft-shoe dance while another little boy played the banjo could coax a smile out of the stoic agent.

Brenna tossed a few coins into the kids' banjo case. Then she spotted the Café du Monde, which she'd just read about in a brochure at the Magnolia Guest House.

"This way." She could already smell the rich coffee and chicory, not to mention the beignets.

"How are you going to treat?" Heath asked. "I thought you were broke."

"I have a little bit of money," she hedged. She didn't want to tell him about the twelve thousand dollars in the lining of her suitcase. With Cindy eloping to Italy for her honeymoon, she would never be able to prove where she'd gotten so much cash.

They lucked out and found a table near the edge of the café, where people-watching was at its best. Brenna dug into her order of beignets, which were light-as-a-cloud, doughnutlike pastries drowning in powdered sugar. They melted in her mouth—she'd never tasted anything so exquisite. She polished hers off in no time, washing them down with the rich coffee, then noticed Heath had only taken a couple of bites of his.

"Don't you like the beignets?"

He made a face. "Too sweet."

"There's no such thing as too sweet." She batted her eyelashes at him, which had the desired effect. He pushed his plate toward her.

"Go for it."

"Thanks." As she savored the last few bites of pure fat and carbs, she pondered her new partner. She was grateful he'd joined forces with her. The prospect of abandoning her pursuit of Marvin had depressed her. But Heath Packer wasn't nearly as much fun as Sonya and Cindy had been. At least with Sonya she could dish about men and clothes and makeup. And Cindy had been just plain fun, with her baby and her puppy and her straightforward way of talking and looking at things.

Heath hardly said a word. He was always at attention, those blue eyes of his darting around on constant alert, as if bad guys were going to accost them at any second.

They would have a lot more fun if he would loosen up a little.

"So where are you from?" she asked. "I know you're not from Texas because of the way you talk, but I can't quite place the accent."

"Most recently from Baltimore."

"What brought you to Dallas? That's where you work out of, right? Dallas?"

"I was transferred there."

"Why? Was it something you requested, or does the FBI move people around arbitrarily?"

"It was a mutual decision."

Brenna's nose quivered. She sensed a story there. "I bet there's a woman involved."

He looked at her sharply. "What makes you say that?"

"Men don't just move halfway across the country for no reason. So, you're running *to* something or *away* from something. I doubt it's anything work related, since you appear to be conscientious about your job. So it must be a woman."

He gave her a look that said she was out of her tree, but he neither confirmed nor denied.

"Okay, I won't pry. I've never been to Baltimore. Is it nice?"

"Yeah, it's a nice city. Pretty harbor. Nice old row houses. Fancy ballpark."

"But not your hometown."

"What makes you say that?"

"There's no passion in your voice. If you'd been born and raised there, you'd either love it or hate it."

He took his time responding, but he finally did. "St. Louis."

Brenna snapped her fingers. "Of course. You've got a midwestern accent, which to me sounds like no accent at all. I spent four years in Kansas City, at the Art Institute. I should have guessed."

"You went to the Kansas City Art Institute?" He seemed surprised.

"I not only went there, I graduated," she said proudly. It was her one tangible success, her single piece of evidence that she wasn't a complete screwup. Her parents hadn't come to her graduation. They hadn't understood what a big deal it was. They thought art school was insignificant compared to law school or business school.

She and Heath lapsed into another silence, and Brenna flipped through a jewelry magazine she'd picked up at one of the stores they'd visited. Suddenly she stopped turning pages. Her heartbeat accelerated. "Oh, my God."

"What?" Heath looked around, his right hand reaching inside his jacket for his gun.

"Back down, there, Mr. FBI man. It's not a physical threat. Take a look at this." She turned the magazine around and showed him the ad that had so captured her attention.

"Synthetic emeralds by mail?"

"Not that ad, this one." She tapped impatiently on the one she meant. "Big gem-and-bead show. This weekend, right here in New Orleans. If I were wanting to unload some hot jewelry fast, that's where I'd do it."

"You think Marvin will be there?"

"I'd bet on it. It's one of those shows where anybody with the money for a booth can exhibit anything they want."

"We'll go, then. The doors open this evening." He paused, regarding her thoughtfully. "How come you didn't know about this show before? You're in the business."

She shrugged. "There are so many shows these days I can't keep track. Besides, once I got accepted to the IJC show, I totally forgot about everything else. I needed all the time I had to get ready for New York. I get a ton of jewelry-trade magazines, but I haven't cracked one in weeks."

"Guess Marvin blew your chances to make a big splash in New York, huh?"

She sighed. "I've been thinking about it. If I pull out of the show, they'll probably never invite me to come back. The IJC is run by a bunch of snobs—cream-of-the-crop designers who want to protect their own positions as top dogs. On the other hand, if I show up with a less-than-stellar collection, they'll also never ask me back."

"So there's no way out?"

"I have to find the stolen jewelry." The more she talked, the more depressed she felt about her situation. "Let's keep working the stores. Somebody, somewhere in this town knows Marvin."

HEATH DIDN'T KNOW what to think about Brenna. Her parents hadn't mentioned anything about a degree from the Kansas City Art Institute, and it hadn't shown up on a background check. That was a pretty decent school. The way the elder Thompsons had presented Brenna, she'd sounded like a dabbler, a hobbyist. But she didn't strike him as that way now.

Then again, what did he know about the jewelry trade?

Fueled by caffeine and sugar, Heath and Brenna visited several more jewelers. But Brenna's enthusiasm waned as afternoon wore into evening. No one recognized Marvin, and there was no sign of the stolen loot.

"Are you ready to go back to your hotel?" Heath asked.

"Yeah. My feet are killing me. Where are you staying? Somewhere fancy? Our tax dollars at work?"

"Actually, I'm in the room next door to yours." But he

would probably spend most of the night in his car, alternating shifts with Grif—who was, speak of the devil, sitting down at a table uncomfortably close, his ubiquitous newspaper in hand. Brenna's back was to Grif, so he grinned and waved at Heath.

Heath suppressed his urge to grin back. Grif was a good guy, fresh out of the academy and still having fun with the job. Heath sighed quietly, remembering when he was like that.

"Gee, and I was going to offer to let you sleep in Sonya's bed," Brenna said breezily. "Without Sonya, I mean. Since she's gone. We could have split the cost of the room."

Heath's breath caught in his throat. Share a room with Brenna? Oh, yeah, that would be a smart move.

"Why would you offer me a place to sleep? I thought you didn't like me."

She batted her eyelashes in that flirty way she had that was starting to drive him crazy. "Well, I *would* like to know whether you wear that tie to bed."

He knew she was flirting to throw him off balance. He clearly wasn't her type. Her father had said she usually dated "long-haired artistic hippie types."

"I don't think the Bureau would go for me sharing a room with a…with a crime victim and potential witness." Damn, he'd almost used the word *suspect*.

"Probably just as well you have your own room." She grinned. "Staying with me, you'd be overwhelmed by my potent sexuality."

She probably had no idea how close to the truth she was.

BRENNA STOPPED OFF at her room to change clothes. The weather in Cottonwood, Texas, had been briskly cool when she and Sonya had taken off last night, but it had degenerated into a muggy eighty degrees in southern Louisiana, unusually warm for November even in New Orleans. Her tank top was damp. She thought about taking a shower, then decided she was too hungry. She'd been ravenous the past few days, even for her.

Heath had suggested she go incognito to the jewelry show, in case Marvin was actually there. The last thing they wanted to do was spook him. She didn't really think Marvin would be dumb enough to show his face at such a public event when he knew he was wanted. He would con someone else—perhaps Miss FrenchQuarterChic—to sell his stuff. Still, after donning a black denim miniskirt and a purple crop top, she tucked her frosted hair into a baseball cap and put on a pair of nonprescription glasses with pale purple lenses, which she sometimes used as eye protection when working with her jewelry. She slid her feet into a pair of platform sandals and freshened her strawberry lip gloss, then left the room.

Heath was waiting for her. Still in his suit. She thought his eyes shone with a strange light when he first looked at her, but then it disappeared—if it was ever there.

"Oh, you look real unobtrusive," she said. "Only maybe four out of five people would guess you were a cop in the first thirty seconds."

He arched one eyebrow at her. "And I suppose you dressed to blend in? Good Lord, have you never heard of a neutral color?"

"I don't own neutral colors. And I've never been the kind to blend. You don't think the hat and glasses are enough? As long as Marvin doesn't get a close look at me, I should be fine."

Heath looked doubtful about that, but he didn't make her

change. They set out toward the New Orleans Convention Center, which was on the river just west of the French Quarter and fortunately only a few blocks from their guest house.

"Where should we go for dinner?" Brenna asked brightly.

"You're hungry *again?*"

"Those beignets were mostly air. Anyway, you must be starving. Hey, how about that place?" She pointed to a dimly lit bar with a corner doorway that looked as if it hadn't changed for fifty years. Smoky jazz filtered out into the street.

"Big Daddy's Oyster Bar?"

"It looks like the sort of place that's not written up in the tourist guides."

"There's probably a reason it's not written up," Heath said dubiously.

"Come on, where's your sense of adventure? This place is just overflowing with local color."

They entered the dark, smoky bar, which listed every kind of oyster dish imaginable on a chalkboard menu as well as boiled crawfish, fried catfish and a bunch of dishes Brenna didn't even recognize.

"Just have a seat any ol' place," the bartender yelled at them. He was an enormous man with a huge belly who could easily have been Big Daddy. "Cherie'll be around to get your order."

Brenna led the way to a cozy booth in a corner, where they had a view of the street as darkness fell. A blues trio played in the back, the smoky strains of bass and guitar wafting through the bar, just loud enough that they could still converse easily.

A beautiful woman with toffee-colored skin and a dress

short enough to get her arrested sauntered up to their table. Her hair was done up in an elaborate style that resembled a pineapple. "What'll it be?"

"I'll have the oyster variety platter and a cold Beck's, if you have one," Brenna said decisively.

The waitress looked at Heath. She licked her lips unconsciously. "How about you, Mr. Cop?"

Heath looked startled, but Brenna just laughed. "Told ya."

"I'll have the étouffée and a Pepsi."

Brenna snorted. "Pepsi?"

"Can't drink on the job, huh?" the waitress said. "You must not be a New Orleans cop, then." She sauntered away, hips swaying.

"You really know how to have fun," Brenna grumbled.

HER COMMENT shouldn't have stung, but it did. Heath used to know how to have fun. He used to have a reputation as laid-back, always ready with a smart comment. He'd shared a great relationship with his fellow agents back in Baltimore. They'd played together in a summer softball league, invited each other over for backyard barbecues.

He'd never been a renegade, exactly, but he hadn't been as worried about the rules as he was now. He'd been the guy people could count on, the one everyone wanted guarding their backs. He'd had a solid reputation for being cool under pressure and closing cases others had given up on.

That was BCA. Before Christine's Arrest.

Now it felt like he was constantly walking on a fragile spiderweb. One false move, and he would break through and plunge into the abyss, or wherever it was that ex-FBI agents went. That, or he would become hopelessly entangled.

He'd made up his mind as soon as he'd learned that his transfer to Dallas was going through—he wasn't going to make that false move. His image at the Bureau was in tatters, and there was only one way to rebuild it, and that was one brick at a time. One arrest, then another. One case solved, then another, and no controversy.

Brenna Thompson was walking controversy. Her irreverence appealed to the old Heath, but that was someone he could no longer afford to be.

He should arrest her and be done with it, he thought for the zillionth time since he'd met her. But that would be too easy. He needed Brenna, Marvin *and* the Picasso.

He had no illusions about what would happen tonight. Brenna wasn't about to knowingly lead him to her accomplice. But she might be planning to make contact, to get a message to Marvin somehow. Heath would be there when she did.

Grif strolled past the restaurant's window for the third time and paused to study the menu posted near the door. The guy was not exactly subtle. Brenna was very observant, and she was going to spot him if he wasn't more careful.

The food arrived, along with Brenna's beer in a frosty mug. Heath's mouth watered. He loved a cold beer as much as the next guy, and it sure would go down good with the spicy shrimp-and-rice dish in front of him. But he could not afford to muddle his thinking or take the edge off his reflexes, even for a moment.

The oyster platter, on the other hand, didn't tempt him in the slightest. He had to look away as Brenna slid the raw ones into her mouth and practically swallowed them whole.

"They're aphrodisiacs, you know," she said lightly.

"That's an old-wives' tale."

"Care to test it out? There's plenty here to share."

"I'll stick to my own meal, thanks." It was pretty good, he had to admit, though his experience with Cajun cuisine was somewhat limited. As for Brenna's flirtation, he didn't take it seriously. "Anyway, I don't need oysters." The words popped out, seemingly of their own accord. He saw he'd at least surprised Brenna, if not shocked her. He'd shocked himself, though he tried real hard not to show it. What had made him say something like that?

How about the truth? All right, so the little blond thief made him hot and bothered like no woman had since he'd outgrown watching the Playboy Channel. That didn't mean he had to act on it. He would just keep his lips zipped from now on—and his pants zipped forever as far as she was concerned.

Brenna polished off her oysters. He wasn't surprised when she wanted dessert. She ordered bread pudding with two spoons and insisted he try a bite. It did smell pretty good, so he dished a little bit onto his spoon, topped off with a smidge of whipped cream and tasted it.

It was heaven, a heady concoction drowning in butter, brown sugar, cinnamon and nutmeg, studded with pecans and topped with a brandy rum sauce. One bite enveloped all of his senses at once. He was even aware of the sound of Brenna licking her lips.

"Too sweet, right?" she said.

"Not this time." He took another bite, then another. Oh, he could get addicted to this in a hurry. Well, hell, this was one sin he could commit without worrying about what Ketcher would think.

By the time they left Big Daddy's Oyster Bar, Heath wished he'd been a bit more circumspect. If he had to suddenly chase a suspect, he wouldn't be able to run half a block.

It was a few more blocks to the convention center, right on the Mississippi River, and Heath was glad for the walk. Once they entered the modern building, crowded with tourists, he felt more at home. Here there were several men in suits. They looked like they might be gem dealers. No one gave him a second look.

Brenna, however, always got a second and sometimes a third or fourth look. Aw, hell, she'd stand out even if she wore a nun's habit. It wasn't how she looked so much as the energy she gave off. She was pure charisma in a pint-size package.

"You're looking forward to this," he observed as they took the elevator up to the third-floor exhibit hall.

"I love looking at jewelry."

"I hadn't guessed." This afternoon he'd almost had to bodily drag her out of several stores. She'd wanted to try on everything, study how it was made, ask questions about the stones. She could tell almost to the year when each piece had been made just by the cut of the gem and the style and color of the setting.

"Remember," he said, "there's no time for browsing or trying stuff on. The ad said there would be hundreds of exhibitors. We need to look through every display for the stolen jewelry. Keep an eye out for Marvin, too. If you see him—"

"I know. Don't confront him. Keep my distance. Leave it to you. Believe me, I learned my lesson in Faring. I'm not going to risk losing him again."

They had to pay a cover charge at the door of the exhibit hall. When they entered, Heath was overwhelmed by the sheer volume of jewelry displayed. He'd never seen so much shiny stuff in one place.

"We need a plan," he said quickly as Brenna immediately darted to the first booth that caught her eye. "Down one row, up another. Let's cover as much territory as we can. Maybe we should split up." If she was planning to meet Marvin, this might be the place. He wanted to give her every opportunity to carry out her plan.

"If we conduct ourselves like generals inspecting the troops, we'll stand out," she said. "We have to amble. We should stick together. You might not recognize my jewelry from the drawings."

Heath was surprised Brenna didn't jump at the chance to split up. If she were truly trying to meet up with Marvin or get a message to him, she would want to get rid of Heath. Once again, he entertained the possibility that he was wrong about her. But how could he be, when the evidence was so condemning?

Evidence could be faked, he reminded himself. He knew Marvin was clever. He could have… No. Heath wasn't going there. Christine had been funny and sexy and very, very lovable. Those qualities had blinded him to the secret life she'd been leading, when the facts had been right in front of him. He wouldn't, couldn't make the same mistake with Brenna. Criminals could be cute and sexy and funny.

They spent close to three hours wending their way down one aisle and another. He had to give Brenna credit, she didn't dawdle. She occasionally asked a question of any exhibitor who seemed to favor contemporary designs, claiming she was looking for a particular kind of sapphire ring to complement an outfit. The ring she described was one of the most distinctive pieces that had been stolen, she'd told Heath earlier, and she was hoping someone might have seen it.

But no one took the bait.

"I think maybe we should quit for the evening," Brenna said suddenly. "I'm not feeling very well."

"I'm not surprised, after all those oysters." But she did look a bit pale, he noted, and a thin sheen of perspiration shimmered on her upper lip.

"Seriously. I need to go back to the Magnolia and lie down or something. We can get an early start in the morning."

"Okay." He was dead on his feet, too. Anyway, it was almost closing time, and most of the exhibitors were securing their spaces for the night.

Brenna headed for the exit. But she'd only taken a few steps when she skidded to a stop. "Oh, my God."

"What? Are you going to be sick?" Heath asked, alarmed.

"Probably. But that's not—" She made a beeline for a nearby exhibitor called French Quarter Chic.

Oh, hell. The lady from the chat room. He couldn't believe he hadn't noticed the sign himself.

MANNING THE BOOTH was a trashy-looking bleached blonde in her late forties with a seventies Farrah Fawcett hairdo. She was chatting with an older man in a cowboy hat, showing him various diamond engagement rings while the much-younger woman at his side squealed and simpered.

Heath cast around for Grif. Where was he?

Brenna rapidly scanned the showcases, then gasped and grabbed Heath's arm. "That's my necklace!" Then, before Heath could even react, she added, "I'm definitely going to be sick." And she bolted for the exit.

Chapter Three

The bleached blonde, whose name tag identified her as Alice Smith, stopped midsentence. "Is there something I can help you with?"

"I'd like to see the opal necklace," he said, indicating the piece Brenna had pointed to. It did resemble one of the sketched designs Brenna had provided when she'd first filed the theft complaint. But did it have Brenna's jeweler's mark? That would be the key to identifying the piece.

"The show is about to close for the night," Alice said, "and I've really got to help this gentleman here. Maybe you could come back tomorrow?"

"I won't be able to do that," he said firmly, finding it highly odd that the woman wouldn't do anything possible to close the sale tonight. He'd seen how eager these exhibitors were to part customers from their cash. "I'd just like to take a quick look at the necklace."

"I can only wait on one customer at a time," she said curtly. "For security reasons." She picked up a can of cola from the table and took a quick gulp from it, then returned her attention to the man in the cowboy hat.

Something didn't feel right here.

Mr. Cowboy Hat stepped aside. "You go ahead and help

this gentleman," he said to Alice. "Delia and I want to talk a bit in private." He handed the ring he'd been looking at back to Alice and walked away.

Hesitating, Alice extracted the pendant from the case and displayed it against her manicured hand, tilting it this way and that to catch the light in a practiced gesture. "You probably just cost me a sale, you know. That guy was about to pull out his platinum American Express."

"Sorry."

He looked closely at the pendant, which featured a round, flat fire opal the size of a nickel, encased in a disc of gold and platinum. It had a sort of Art Deco feel to it, but modern, too. Very clean lines.

"Where did this come from?" he asked casually.

"An estate sale in Florida. I've had it for a few months, but it needed repairs. This is the first I've shown it. Several people have said they might come back for it, so if you're interested…"

Heath held out his hand. "May I?"

The woman handed it across the table to him. He casually flipped over the pendant. He didn't see Brenna's mark. He examined the piece with his jeweler's loupe. No sign of her name. No mark of any kind.

"Do you know who the designer is?" he asked.

"No."

"Do you have a receipt for it?"

Alice's face hardened. "What's this about?"

"The woman who was with me a moment ago thinks the necklace might be stolen. From her."

Alice's face melted into an expression of sympathy and her demeanor changed abruptly. "That's awful. Oh, I hope it's not true. I have the receipt in my office at home, I'm sure. I could get it for you. The outfit I bought it from is a respectable company that runs estate sales all over northern Florida. I can't imagine they would deal in stolen merchandise. When did the theft occur?"

"Only a few weeks ago."

Alice smiled. "Well then, it couldn't be the same piece. If you want to give me your fax number, I can fax the receipt to you." She handed Heath a card.

AliceSmith224@coolmail.com.

"Do you go by FrenchQuarterChic on the Internet?" he asked.

"No," she answered, hard and swift. She held her hand out, obviously wanting her necklace back. "I really need to get going. I have to pick up my grandkid at the babysitter's before it gets too late."

Heath handed back the necklace. Could it be a coincidence? Maybe Brenna had been mistaken. Her mark wasn't anywhere on the pendant. He decided the only way to sort this out was to bring Brenna herself back here to take a closer look at the piece.

Where the hell was Grif? When he really needed the guy, he was MIA.

He flashed his badge at Alice, whose eyes widened. "I don't want you to leave this spot until I get back. I'm going to assume, for now, that it's all a mistake. But if I have to come looking for you—and I will—I'll have a whole new set of assumptions, and they won't be pretty. Understood?"

"Well, you don't have to get nasty," she grumbled. "But I'm not waiting here all night."

She didn't intimidate easily, he thought as he took off after Brenna.

The security guard at the door had noticed Brenna, who didn't exactly blend into the crowd. At Heath's question, he pointed out the direction she'd taken—down a corridor that led to the ladies' room. The corridor was empty. He cracked open the ladies' room swinging door. "Brenna?"

"Leave me alone," she called back on a moan.

"Are you okay?"

"What do you think?"

Hoping no one else was in there, he entered, holding his FBI shield just in case. But the room was deserted. Amazing, given how busy the trade show was.

He found Brenna leaning over the sink, splashing cold water on her face. She raised up, looking at him in the mirror, then blotted her face with a paper towel.

"Get out. This is a ladies' bathroom, for gosh sake."

"I was worried about you."

"I'm fine. Go arrest somebody. That woman had my necklace."

"Are you sure? You didn't look at it very closely."

"Of course I'm sure! You think I can't recognize a piece of jewelry I worked over for days?"

"I looked it over. It doesn't have your mark."

That stopped her. "You're sure?"

"Positive."

"Marvin could have removed the mark."

"The woman said she bought the piece six months ago in Florida."

"Then she was lying! Heath, did you just let her walk away?"

"I flashed my badge and told her not to leave. If you look at the necklace and positively identify it as yours, I can demand that she produce the receipt."

"Let's go, then."

"Are you sure you're okay?"

"I'll live. Freaking oysters," she muttered. "And I don't want to hear you even *think* 'I told you so.'"

He wouldn't say it, that was for sure. He felt too sorry for her to add to her misery. But he was thinking it.

She looked shaky as they headed back for the exhibit hall. Fearing she might fall off her platform shoes, he offered her his arm, but she shook her head.

It was after ten, and the show was officially closed now. The security guard at the door let them in only when Heath flashed his badge. But as soon as they got inside the exhibit hall, Heath realized he'd made a terrible mistake. The French Quarter Chic booth was empty. Alice was gone, and so were all of her display cases.

The booths on either side of her were also deserted. Queries to a couple of other exhibitors were useless; everyone was focused on securing their own merchandise for the evening.

He left Brenna on a padded bench by the door, whispered to the guard not to let her go anywhere, then located the show's security chief, who was concerned and cooperative. He enlisted a handful of his men to search for Alice, but she'd disappeared like a snake slithering into a pond, not even leaving a ripple. He personally searched her space, finding nothing but her empty soft drink can.

Supremely disappointed, he headed back toward where he'd left Brenna. Grif suddenly appeared by his side. "What happened?"

"Where were you?" Heath demanded.

"I stopped to buy some earrings for my girlfriend." He patted his shirt pocket. "You seemed to have everything under control."

"Yeah, well, all hell broke loose." Heath stopped himself before he could lose his temper. He was irritated with Grif, but more angry with himself. He never should have let Alice get away. But he'd allowed his concern for Brenna's welfare interfere with his good judgment.

He filled in Grif, who let loose with some suitably colorful curses. Then he asked, "What now?"

"I'll take Brenna back to her room. She's really sick. I don't think she'll be getting into trouble tonight, so you can go catch some sleep if you want." He handed Grif Alice's empty soft drink can, which he'd placed in a small labeled sack. "And if you could drop this by the lab on your way home—"

"No problem. You're sure Brenna's not faking?"

No one could turn that shade of gray on purpose. "I'm sure."

"I'll come back about four, then, to relieve you." He paused. "I'm really sorry, man."

Heath couldn't stay mad at Grif. "Hope your girl really likes those earrings."

Brenna was where he'd left her. She gave him an accusing look. "You didn't find her, did you."

"No. Brenna, I couldn't arrest her without stronger proof. If you could have positively identified—"

"I did!"

"But your mark—"

"Could have been filed off."

"We'll find her," he promised. He had high hopes for finding prints on the can.

"I just want to go to bed," Brenna said miserably.

"Let's go, then."

There was no way Brenna was up to walking the ten blocks back to her guest house. The taxi line in front of the convention center was thirty deep, too.

"Just lay me down in the gutter," Brenna said. "I'll be fine."

Then Heath saw something that might be their salvation. He sat Brenna down on another bench, placed her purse in her lap and crossed her arms over it. New Orleans seethed with purse snatchers and pickpockets, and a sick young woman would be a handy target. "I'll be back in a minute. Don't move."

"As if I could."

Brenna wanted to die. Really, truly. She'd never felt so sick in her life. Then again, she'd never eaten a dozen tainted oysters, for surely that was the problem. But did food poisoning come with a fever? She was sweating and shivering at the same time, and her stomach threatened to revolt again at any moment.

She slumped down and put her head in her hands. Thank God she'd made it to the bathroom before. She'd die of embarrassment if she threw up in front of Heath. She supposed people barfing in the street was a commonplace thing in New Orleans, but it wasn't something she intended to do.

The clip-clop of a horse's hooves drew her attention. She looked up to see one of the French Quarter's horse and carriages pulling up right in front of her. The horse wore a festive yellow hat with orange flowers.

Heath hopped down from the carriage. "I found us some wheels."

"You have got to be kidding."

"It's this or I carry you back to your hotel."

She actually smiled at that thought. Heath held out his hand, and she surprised herself by taking it. Moments earlier she'd wanted to strangle Heath for letting that thieving jeweler get away. But now she was oddly touched by the way he was taking care of her. He could have simply abandoned her, let her find her own way back to her guest house.

She was so weak she could hardly pull herself into the

high carriage. But between Heath and the driver, they hoisted her up. She didn't miss the fact that Heath put his hand on her bottom to accomplish the feat. She didn't miss the fact that, even in her debilitated condition, she liked it. She wondered if he'd peeked up her short skirt.

Heath climbed in beside her and the carriage took off.

"You're shivering." He took off his suit jacket and put it around her.

"Th-think I have a fever." Her teeth chattered. Heath put his arm around her. His body felt warm, and she snuggled into it. Oh, Lord, he smelled great.

Between the gentle rocking of the carriage and the hypnotic clip-clop of the horse's hooves, she fell asleep. The next thing she knew, she was being carried up the outside stairs to her room. And it was Heath carrying her.

"Oh, for gosh sake, put me down," she protested feebly. "I can walk."

"Hush. We're almost there now, anyway." When he reached her door he set her down, fished around in her small purse until he found a key and opened the door.

The room was freezing. She'd left the air-conditioning on. Heath walked across to the window unit and flipped it off. Then he yanked back the covers. "Get in."

"I need a shower."

"Only if you want me in there with you, holding you up."

He was right. She was about to fall down. Her stomach felt like a giant hand was squeezing it like one of those stress balls, and she was so dizzy she was swaying. She took two steps, crawled across the bed and dropped.

Heath took off her sandals, covered her with the blankets. "I have some medicine in my bag, down in my car. I'll be right back."

While he was gone, she managed to wiggle out of her uncomfortably damp clothes and pull the covers over herself. Oh, God, why couldn't she just die? It would be so much easier.

Heath returned a few minutes later and held out a handful of pills. "Something for nausea, something for pain and fever, and a muscle relaxer. Should knock you right out."

"You always travel with a pharmacy?"

"I can't afford to be sick in the middle of a job."

She wasn't sure how well the pills would sit on her beleaguered stomach, but she swallowed them with the water Heath brought her, then snuggled down deeper under the thin covers. "I'll be okay," she said. "You can go."

"I don't think so. I'm on the razor's edge of taking you to the hospital."

"No." But she realized she was in no condition to fight him, if that's what he wanted to do. "Stay, then. But if this is just a clever ploy to get a free bed for the night, forget it. You're gonna have to pay for half…the room." Already, a pleasant lethargy was taking over her. Whether the muscle relaxer was working or simple exhaustion was taking over, she thought maybe she'd drop off again. Even if Heath Packer was watching her and she might drool in her sleep.

Her last conscious thought was that, no, he didn't sleep in his tie. And he wore surprisingly sexy underwear for such a straitlaced guy.

BRENNA WAS SICK almost all night, off and on. She managed to doze off between bouts of violent retching.

By morning, however, the worst seemed to be over. She was awakened by the sound of her hotel room door opening. She cracked open one eye and saw Heath Packer entering, one tall paper cup in each hand.

She groaned and hid her head under the covers. Heath Packer had spent the night in her hotel room, but had she managed to make the best of the situation? No, of course not. He'd seen her sick and sweating and half-delirious and, yes, probably drooling.

He managed to close the door quietly with his foot, then set the two cups on the nightstand. That's when he spotted her peering at him with one eye, most of the rest of her under the covers.

"Hey." He smiled, not unkindly. "What's the story? Are you going to live?"

"I'm not sure. Did you spend the night in here?"

He pointed to the other bed, tellingly rumpled. "Part of the night."

"Do you wear skimpy black bikini underwear, or did I dream that part? I'd have guessed you were a tighty-whitey guy all the way."

"I have no idea what you're talking about."

Maybe she'd dreamed it after all. At any rate, he was back in his suit pants today, paired with another crisp, white shirt. No tie, though. His dark hair was neatly combed, his face freshly shaved.

"Do you want breakfast?" he asked, indicating a white bakery bag.

She groaned melodramatically and hid under the covers again. "Don't you dare show me any food. Whatever it is, I don't want to see it or smell it."

"Okay. But it's just some dry toast. That's supposed to be good for an upset stomach. I brought you some hot tea with honey, too."

Was this guy for real? Most men ran the other way when anyone around them took ill. Her father once left the house for three days when her mother had the flu.

She figured Heath was probably being so nice because he'd realized he needed her. She was the one who'd spotted the stolen necklace. She was the one who'd come up with French Quarter Chic. For all the good it had done.

"I might try the tea," she finally said, deciding a couple of sips wouldn't kill her. If she kept those down, maybe she would get really wild and take a bite of toast.

She started to sit up, then abruptly remembered she'd taken off all her clothes last night. She peeked under the covers and relaxed when she realized she had on her old, tattered flannel nightgown, the one she'd shoved to the bottom of the suitcase in embarrassment after she saw the matching-nightie-and-peignoir sets Sonya favored.

Wait a minute. No matter how debilitated she'd been, she would never have chosen to put this on when there was a handsome guy in the room.

She sat up and shot Heath a suspicious glare as he removed the top from her tea and handed it to her. "You didn't, um…" No. That was ridiculous.

"Did you want milk for your tea?" he asked, thinking that was the problem.

"Did you put me in a nightgown last night?" she blurted out.

"You were shivering. That was the warmest thing I could find in your suitcase," he said matter-of-factly.

She knew her face must be flaming. She was going to die of embarrassment. She took a gulp of tea to hide her discomfort. Though she didn't much care for tea, this was good—hot, strong and sweet.

"Take it easy," Heath cautioned. He took his own cup, which apparently contained coffee, and pulled off the lid. Then he settled back on his bed with the morning paper.

Gee, wasn't this cozy?

"You saw me naked," she couldn't help pointing out.

He looked up. "What?"

"You saw me naked."

He grinned. "I didn't look. Not that I wasn't tempted, but I'm not the kind of guy who takes advantage of a woman when she's down."

"How could you not look?"

He rolled his eyes. "I handed the nightgown to you. I turned my back. You put it on."

Brenna knew she should have been relieved. She was disappointed instead. Not that she would have been at her fetching best last night. *More like my retching best.* She wished she could remember. If she'd been naked in front of Heath Packer, she ought to be able to remember it.

She forced herself to focus on something else. She drank more of the hot, sweet tea, then forced down a couple of bites of the dry toast. Her stomach didn't seem to mind it.

"I think a shower might do me some good." She retreated to the bathroom, bringing some fresh clothes with her. She was pitifully weak. But by the time she dressed and brushed her teeth, she was feeling almost human again. She pulled on a lime-green tank top and a pair of electric blue pants with a beaded design running down the side seams.

It took lots of makeup to disguise that sickly prison pallor and puffy eyes, and half a bottle of styling gel to spike her hair just right. But by the time she was finished, she thought she looked pretty hot. Well, pretty okay. Not that her cold-fish roommate would notice. Jeez, if he could see her naked and be totally unaffected, she was losing her touch.

As soon as Brenna went into the bathroom, Heath quit pretending to read the paper and put it down. Hell, yes, he'd put the nightgown on her. The poor woman's teeth had been chattering so loudly she'd been in danger of cracking a molar. But contrary to what he'd just told her, he'd had to dress her himself. She'd been groggy from the muscle relaxer and half-delirious with fever.

He had definitely looked.

Then he'd covered her with every blanket in the room. And when she was still shivering, he'd gotten into bed with her and added his own body heat to the prescription.

After a few minutes the shivering had stopped and she'd dropped into a more normal sleep. Praying she wouldn't remember any of it, he'd reluctantly slid out of her bed and into his own to catch some sleep.

Unfortunately, he remembered her every contour, exactly what it felt like to have her bottom tucked up against his very hard arousal, her shoulders pressed against his chest, the soft give of her flesh beneath the tattered flannel as he'd wrapped his arms around her. The feel of her would be with him always, he was sure.

Thank God she didn't seem to recall.

Chapter Four

By noon Brenna claimed she felt well enough to leave the hotel room. "I really can't stand being cooped up in here anymore," she said. "I want to take action. Marvin's out there somewhere."

"He probably knows we're on to him," Heath pointed out. "He'll go underground again. He might already be halfway to another city, another state."

"Well, aren't *you* the bluebird of happiness."

"Just trying to be realistic."

"So are you saying we should give up?"

"No." Heath was ambivalent about actually finding Marvin Carter. Because the minute he did, he would have to arrest Brenna. Every cell in his body told him that would be the wrong thing to do. Of course, his instincts could no longer be trusted. He had to remind himself of that on an hourly basis.

Brenna applied some cotton-candy pink lipstick and a bit of blush. Wearing Doc Martens and a baggy pair of bright blue pants that rode so low he wondered how they stayed up, she declared herself ready for action.

"So put on your tie and let's go," she urged him.

"I'm not wearing the tie today."

She looked shocked. "No?"

"No." He'd taken enough grief from her about that. But he'd slid one into his jacket pocket, just in case.

"What's the plan?"

"Do you like picture books?"

Brenna gave him a blank look, and he grinned. A few minutes later, they were seated at a New Orleans police station, thumbing through books of mug shots.

"Maybe she's not even in the system," Brenna said. "She might be just some gullible patsy Marvin is using."

"She looked me in the eye last night and lied through her capped teeth. And she ensured well ahead of time that she couldn't be traced through her paperwork from the show. You don't acquire criminal instincts overnight."

But after two hours they hadn't spotted her. Brenna's mood was low as they left the police station. "Do you want some lunch?" he asked, nodding a silent acknowledgment to Grif, sitting in his car reading a newspaper.

She shook her head.

"Oh, come on. You're really not hungry?"

"Well, I guess I could eat some crackers or something. But let's try to find someplace that doesn't serve seafood. If I even get a whiff of oysters…"

"Enough said."

They found a sandwich place where they could sit outside and watch boat traffic on the Mississippi. Heath got a hamburger and fries. Brenna ordered plain, boiled white rice.

"That's all you want, sugar?" the waitress asked.

Brenna nodded. After the waitress left, she stared moodily out at the river. "It's hell to be in a place like New Orleans and not be able to eat."

"For you, I imagine so." But he couldn't help smiling

at her. She was like an exuberant puppy that had suddenly run out of energy. He wanted to cuddle her. He wanted to do more than that.

She's a thief, you idiot. No matter how many times he told himself that, it didn't feel right. But the evidence was irrefutable. He'd seen with his own eyes the confession note she'd written. He had it memorized:

Dear Mom and Dad,
Let me say first that I love you, and I've never stopped loving you. I'm not sure how we got to this place where we can't even talk. I suppose I'm crazy for believing I can make things right with some grand gesture, but I've got to try. I'm sorry, I'm just so sorry—

The note had been handwritten on her personalized stationery and pinned to the blank wall where the Picasso painting had hung in the Thompsons' living room. Although she hadn't signed it, the FBI crime lab's handwriting expert had verified that the writing was Brenna's.

Two Picassos had been stolen that night—a preparatory drawing, and the painting that had resulted from it, of a girl giving milk to a cat. They were early works, before the artist had started scrambling body parts. By itself, the drawing was worth maybe thirty thousand dollars, the painting at least a million. Together, they were worth much more.

The drawing had been found under Brenna's bed in her loft apartment. Heath had been there for the search.

Still, even with such convincing evidence of her guilt, he just couldn't see it. He'd even toyed with ways in which Marvin might have framed Brenna. He could have planted the drawing in her loft, but it seemed unlikely, since giv-

ing up the drawing would dramatically decrease the value
of the painting. And the note—there was no way he could
have reproduced that note.

Heath's cell phone rang when he was halfway through
his burger. It was the call he'd been dreading, from Fleming Ketcher.

"What in the hell is going on with you?" were the first
words out of Ketcher's mouth.

Heath nodded an apology to Brenna and left the table,
making his way to the end of the deck area where the tables were empty and no one could overhear.

"I'm trying to conduct an investigation," Heath said
evenly, though Ketcher had the ability to make Heath's
blood boil just by opening his mouth. He had that effect
on a lot of people. In fact, he was known as the biggest ty-
rant in the Bureau. Agents who worked under him were always requesting transfers, which was why Heath had
ended up working under Ketcher. Punishment. He figured
the high-up muckety-mucks were hoping Heath would
quit.

"Where's the Thompson girl?" Ketcher wanted to know.

"She's eating rice about thirty feet away from me. I
haven't let her out of my sight, though she has no idea she's
under suspicion. She thinks she's helping me catch Marvin."

"I don't understand the delay," Ketcher said peevishly.
"Just bring her in. A couple of hours of interrogation and
she'd squash like a grape. We'd get faster, better results
than all this cloak-and-dagger stuff of yours."

"I'm making progress," Heath insisted. He told Ketcher about Alice, and the fact that Brenna had identified a
piece of the jewelry she claimed was stolen from her.

"So?" Ketcher said. "She could have pointed to *anything* and claimed it was hers."

"But this piece did look like one of the drawings she gave us." Well, sort of. Then Heath went on to explain Alice's suspicious behavior, and the fact she was a phony from the word go. "The lab here is working on the fingerprint she left behind," Heath said. "Let me at least follow up on that. She might very well be an associate of Marvin Carter's."

Ketcher gave a long-suffering sigh. "Keep me updated." He hesitated, then added, "This Brenna Thompson. Attractive, yes?"

Heath didn't like where this conversation was going. "A little on the bizarre side, but yeah, she's no dog." He figured if he lied, Ketcher would know. Brenna's high school graduation picture was in her file. She'd had long, dark hair back then, but she'd still been a stunner.

"Is there any reason I should worry?" Ketcher asked casually. "Given your history, I mean." He almost sounded apologetic.

Heath ground his teeth together. He longed to simply hang up on his boss, to not dignify the question with an answer. But he was committed to playing by the book, acting the model FBI agent. "No, there is absolutely no reason to worry."

BRENNA FELT ANXIOUS waiting for Heath to return to the table. She'd sneaked a few looks at him as he'd spoken to whoever had called, hoping it was news about fingerprints. But she could tell by the look on his face and his tense posture and balled fists that this was not good news.

"Everything okay?" she asked when he came back.

"Peachy." He didn't volunteer anything else, just finished his hamburger in silence.

Brenna ate her rice one delicate forkful at a time. She was starting to feel hungry and would have liked something less bland. But she didn't trust her stomach, and she was not going to embarrass herself again.

Heath paid the bill. As they waited for his credit card to be processed, his phone rang again. This time he didn't leave the table. He pulled a notebook from his pocket and scribbled a few things down, then disconnected the call.

"We have an ID on the woman and an address. Her name's Ardith Smelter and she's been arrested three times for possession of stolen property."

"She's a fence!" Brenna declared triumphantly. She enjoyed tossing around the lingo she was picking up from Heath. "Then why wasn't she in the mug book?"

"She probably was. With different hair, different teeth, no makeup, we could have missed her." Heath scribbled his name on the credit card receipt. "Let's go."

They picked up Heath's big FBI-mobile, consulted a map and drove to the Garden District. Ardith lived in a carriage house behind a stately, white-columned mansion. Heath parked discreetly at the curb in front of the house next door while they waited for backup to arrive. Finally a blue Jeep Cherokee pulled up behind them and a young blond man got out. Brenna stared and stared at him. Where had she seen him before? Well, maybe he just had one of those faces.

To Brenna's supreme disappointment, the two agents made her wait in the car. She watched out the car window, however, as Heath and the blond man knocked on the carriage house door. No one answered. It appeared no one was there.

Brenna sighed. She was primed for action. She wanted to pounce on the woman, pin her down, demand to know where Marvin was. And she wanted her necklace back. Did Ardith Smelter have more of Brenna's pieces? If she could even recover a few, she might be able to exhibit at the IJC show.

The two men tried the main house, but no one was home there, either. Heath returned to the car. "We're going to wait awhile, see if anyone shows up."

Brenna was not good at waiting. But the other agent, whose name was Grif, was a charming guy who entertained her with stories about the FBI Academy and all the mistakes he'd made as a green recruit.

But after a while, even Grif's patter slowed down. As they sat in the steamy car, watching the street, Brenna fidgeted.

"How are you feeling?" Heath asked solicitously.

"Oh, all right, I guess. I just hate doing nothing. Could we take a walk? Just to the end of the block."

Heath shrugged. "I guess it wouldn't hurt to stretch our legs."

Grif stayed behind. He stretched out in the backseat and closed his eyes.

"He's not really sleeping, is he?" Brenna asked Heath as they walked slowly down to one end of the block. "I mean, surely that's not allowed, sleeping on a surveillance."

"I doubt he's sleeping."

Brenna couldn't help but admire the beautiful antebellum homes, surrounded by lush foliage and blooming flowers, even in November. She'd always fancied herself a natural-born urban dweller. She liked being in the middle of a noisy city, with traffic and sirens. But this neighborhood had a definite appeal. She could see herself in one of these gorgeous houses, enjoying her morning coffee on a wide balcony, watching the birds and the squirrels. She could turn the carriage house into her studio.

"Where do you live?" she asked Heath, who had lapsed into his customary silence. "What part of Dallas, I mean?"

"Addison."

She wrinkled her nose at the mention of one of her least-favorite suburbs. Addison was almost nothing but chain restaurants and cloned apartment complexes. "You like it there?"

"It's okay. The Bureau picked out the apartment. I always thought I'd buy a condo once I got to know the city, but I haven't gotten around to it."

"There are still some spaces left in my building," she said, more to get his reaction than anything. She was pretty sure Heath Packer wasn't the downtown loft type—especially not one like hers, which wasn't in one of those swanky, redeveloped buildings. It was just an old brick structure with some tired-looking businesses on the first floor and four floors above that used to be offices. When the owner could no longer rent out the outdated spaces, and no one wanted to buy the entire building, he started selling it out in parcels. He didn't do a lick of work—he left that to the new owners. That was how Brenna had been able to afford to live there.

Heath surprised her by asking, "What do they sell for?"

"Dirt cheap."

"Well, that area's not exactly the city's showplace."

She wondered how he knew that. She hadn't told him precisely where her building was. But he was with the FBI, she reminded herself. He probably had done a thorough check on her before he'd followed her to Cottonwood.

"The neighborhood's not as bad as it looks," she said. "A little rough around the edges. But the city's best deli is right around the corner, and next door to it is an Italian place to die for."

"If it has good restaurants close by, what else does it need?"

"I think I'm being made fun of."

He flashed one of his rare smiles, and her heart did a funny little hippety-hop. Of all the inappropriate men for her to get a crush on! And that's all it was, she told herself. An adolescent crush. He was a big, bad FBI agent, yet he'd been kind to her when she was ill. And he was, after all, trying to help her recover her jewelry.

She'd never been attracted to a strong, silent type before. Normally she couldn't stand a man who wouldn't talk. She was continually taking in the sensitive-artist types who opened up to her and told her their innermost feelings. Of course, none of those relationships lasted longer than about three weeks, or the time it took for her to get tired of the guy sleeping in her place rent-free and mooching food off her while waiting to be discovered.

Marvin, in the guise of Seneca Dealy, had been refreshingly self-sufficient, the first guy to pay attention to her who seemed to have his life already together. He hadn't needed her to fix him. He'd wanted to fix *her.* But he'd been a talker. Though he'd listened when she needed to spill her guts, he'd also talked a lot about how he was going to fulfill all Brenna's dreams. Such big plans.

Maybe a nontalker was what she needed after all. Someone who would just *be* with her, instead of pulling or pushing at her.

She stole a sideways glance at Heath, noting his strong profile and square Dick Tracy jaw, the intelligent eyes. Her heart gave another one of those peculiar flutters.

What a hoot—her and an FBI agent.

Not that it would ever happen. Heath had shown no inclination toward her, other than an occasional hormonal surge.

They'd just reached the car when a red PT Cruiser sped up the street and careened into the driveway of the house they'd been watching. Grif was out of the car in an instant, proving he hadn't been sleeping on the job after all.

Heath abruptly changed direction and headed up the driveway where the red car had parked. The person behind the wheel was clearly a male, not their suspect, so he didn't object when Brenna followed. They all three caught up with the car's driver, an Asian man in his twenties, very trendy looking, a cigarette dangling from his lips.

"Hi," Heath said with a disarming smile. "Sorry to bother you, but we're looking for an Ardith Smelter. We were given this address." He nodded toward the carriage house.

The Asian man gave them a blank look. "No one lives here but me."

He was too young to be Ardith's live-in, Brenna concluded, and chances were slim he was related by blood. Her heart sank.

"Have you been here long?" Heath asked.

"'Bout three years."

Brenna's heart reached her knees.

"Oh," the other man said suddenly, "maybe you're talking about the lady who lived here before me. I met her once. Older lady, blonde?"

Heath nodded encouragingly.

"You might ask my landlady," the man offered helpfully. "Maybe she has a forwarding address or something."

But the landlady turned out to be a dead end. She arrived home about five minutes after her tenant. She confirmed that Ardith Smelter had lived in her carriage house, but she'd moved out three years ago and hadn't left a forwarding address.

Heath thanked the woman for her cooperation. Then he and Brenna walked back to the car.

Brenna's feet felt like lead. She hadn't realized how many hopes she'd been pinning on finding Ardith Smelter until they failed.

Heath thanked Grif for his help, and Grif took off.

"He seems young to be an FBI agent," Brenna commented. "And he looks so familiar."

"He has one of those faces," Heath said dismissively, clearly not wanting to talk about Grif.

"What do we do now?" she asked glumly as Heath turned on the ignition. The Buick's air-conditioning quickly kicked into gear. Brenna put her flushed face right in front of the vent.

"We could eat again."

Brenna surprised herself by laughing. "I think I'm a bad influence on you. Yesterday you didn't seem interested in food at all."

"Yesterday I had an agenda. When I'm working a case, I forget to eat. When the pressure eases up, I make up for it."

"Are you calling it quits, then?"

"I'm afraid so. We have no leads left to follow in New Orleans. I can make some inquiries about Smelter with the local police, and we can flag her Social Security number. But if she's using a false identity, or more than one, she'll be hard to catch."

"What about Marvin? Are you tracking his Social Security number?"

"We don't have one. We're not even sure who he is."

"But his name really is Marvin Carter," Brenna said. "It was on his car registration."

"Do you have any idea how many Marvin Carters there

are in this country? Before I followed you to New Orleans, I checked out dozens of them from all over the country, everyone from the heir to a Boston financial empire to a homeless man in San Francisco. I can't find anything that matches up with—"

"Wait a minute. The heir to a Boston financial empire. That was the story he gave Sonya. Maybe it's true!"

"His MO is to claim the identities of real people. Seneca Dealy was a real art agent. Dexter Shalimar, the name he used with Cindy, is an actual real estate developer."

Brenna was impressed. Heath had never talked to her about the investigation. She'd assumed all he'd done was follow her around. "You really have been working hard on this case."

"Harder than you know."

She didn't understand exactly what he meant by that cryptic remark, but she sensed a sadness in him. She felt a grudging respect for him, for the fact that he took his job seriously enough to feel bad when he failed. All the other law-enforcement types she'd encountered since this sojourn had begun—with the exception of Deputy Rheems in Cottonwood—had taken a more "win some, lose some" approach. She didn't feel quite so alone with Heath on her side.

They stopped at a coffee shop to get something cold to drink and use the facilities. The shop had an old-fashioned lunch counter, so they sat on the red vinyl stools to sip their drinks and figure out what to do next.

Brenna looked at her watch. "It's after five."

"Yeah?"

"So, if the case is at a dead end and there's no more work to do, you get to clock out, right? I mean, the Bureau doesn't expect you to work 24/7, do they?"

"Actually, they do," he said with a grin.

"Tonight you're clocking out," she declared. "If we're going to go home tomorrow with our tails between our collective legs, we can at least have a night in the French Quarter to commemorate our failed manhunt, right?"

"Uh…"

"We're in New Orleans, Heath! We may never get back here. Let's make the most of it!"

"Are you feeling up to it?"

"I'm feeling great!" She wasn't really. Her stomach was still a bit wobbly, and her head spun every time she stood up. But she figured a square meal—one that didn't feature tainted seafood—would put her back at a hundred percent. Anyway, she was willing to give it a try. Since Heath was returning home tomorrow, she would, too. She had no more solid leads and no desire to continue the investigation alone. No way was she going to spend her last night in New Orleans hunkered down in her hotel room.

"All right," he said, almost resignedly. Then, with more conviction, "All right. We'll make a night of it."

Chapter Five

Heath knew he was in serious trouble when he saw the tiny red dress Brenna pulled out of her suitcase. She put it on a hanger. He knew the minute he agreed to a night out on the town with Brenna that it was a big mistake, a huge mistake.

Let's see. He had two choices. Arrest his suspect and haul her to Dallas for interrogation. Or take her out for dinner and sightseeing. Now which choice would a good FBI agent make? Which one would look better on his record? Which choice would help restore his bruised reputation? And which was likely to simply add more bruises?

Maybe the powers that be were right. Maybe he had a fatal weakness for pretty, sexy felons that rendered him incapable of doing his job.

"I'm just going to hang this up in the bath while I shower," Brenna said cheerfully. "The wrinkles will steam right out."

"Mmm," Heath said noncommittally, picturing Brenna in the shower. He didn't even try to suppress the image this time.

If he just had a lead, even a thin one, he could delay the moment he would have to arrest Brenna. He wanted to give her her night on the town, some memories she could linger over while riding to Dallas in the backseat of his car, handcuffed. It turned his stomach just thinking about it.

He should touch base with Grif.

He knocked on the bathroom door and opened it a crack, noting that she trusted him enough that she didn't even lock the door. "Brenna?"

She turned the faucets off. "What? Did you say something?"

"Yeah. I'm going out. I'll be back to get you in an hour or so, okay?"

"Sure, okay."

Grif was lounging in his Jeep partially hidden by a large magnolia tree, windows open, reading a magazine. But he must have been watching, because he put down the magazine long before Heath reached the car.

"What's the plan, Stan?" Grif asked easily.

"There isn't one. That's the problem. She isn't going to lead us to Marvin or the stolen painting. I'm out of leads."

"Bummer. I was counting on this gig to last a few more days."

"Enjoying it?"

"Who wouldn't? Watching Brenna Thompson all day and all night isn't what I call hard duty. So, you gonna do it now?"

"I guess. She's in the shower right now. She thinks we're going for a night of carousing in the French Quarter before we head home in defeat."

"She has no idea you're about to whip out the handcuffs, huh?"

"None at all."

"Bummer," Grif said again. Then he thought a moment. "You know, I think she might be planning to meet this Marvin tonight."

"You do?" Heath was appalled to realize how desperate he was for any thread to cling to, anything to delay the inevitable. "Why? Did you see something?"

"I, uh, saw her make a phone call."

"When?" Heath asked suspiciously. He'd been with Brenna every second today. Well, except…

"While you were in the bathroom at that coffee shop. I think I might have overheard her say 'Marvin' and 'French Quarter' and 'meet me tonight.'"

Heath shook his head. "Very funny."

Grif chuckled. "Seriously, dude, why would you want to arrest her now? You'll just have to drive half the night to get her back to Dallas, then you'll be up the rest of the night processing her."

"What's in it for you if I wait?" Heath asked, sensing his temporary partner had an agenda in mind.

"I have a date tonight. I was going to show her a good time by taking her on a stakeout. She really gets off on this macho FBI stuff. Plain ol' dinner and a movie aren't going to get me laid, know what I mean?"

Unfortunately, he did.

"So just pretend we have another lead," Grif said. "I'll back you up. Besides, you can't tell me you wouldn't enjoy taking Brenna out, buying her a few drinks…" He let his voice trail off.

Oh, boy.

"Let her have her night on the town," Grif wheedled. "And while you're at it, loosen up, yourself. This job sucks most of the time. Tonight, for a few hours, it won't suck. Think of it that way."

It was the worst advice Heath had ever heard. He grabbed it like a drowning swimmer tossed a life preserver.

HEATH SHOWERED and dressed with care in the only clothes he'd brought that didn't scream FBI—khaki slacks and a loud print shirt. He threw a linen jacket on to cover the shoulder holster, and loafers with no socks. When he looked in the mirror, he decided that all he needed was a two-day growth of beard to be very *Miami Vice*.

He used to dress like this all the time, and he caught hell for it, too. The more his superiors in Baltimore had complained, the louder Heath's shirts had become.

That was all BCA, or Before Christine's Arrest, when his job had still been fun.

He returned to Brenna's room and tapped lightly. He'd given her more than an hour, which seemed plenty of time for any woman to get ready for anything.

She opened the door, then walked back to her bed doing a funny duck-walk. He realized she had a strange-looking rubber appliance wedged between her toes.

"I just polished my toenails," she said by way of explanation. "They're not quite dry."

"No hurry," he said. "We're going to be fashionably early for dinner as it is."

"Mmm, I don't care. I'm actually hungry, and I never thought I'd be hungry again."

Heath inhaled deeply. The room smelled fantastic, of lotion and nail polish and the strawberry-scented shampoo he saw earlier in the bathroom. He detected the scent of lip gloss.

The combination of scents was uniquely Brenna, and it made his chest tighten. It made other places a tad tight, too.

He finally allowed himself to look fully at Brenna, who was studiously blowing on her toenails. She had both feet up on the bed, knees to her chest, the amazing little red dress clinging so tightly to her thighs that she showed nothing she shouldn't.

Her hair was the spikiest he'd seen it yet, the bright blond contrasting with an inch of dark roots. He had no idea why that look was so sexy. Maybe it was because in high school, when his formative sexual desires had first sprung, girls who bleached their hair were baaaaad girls. And bad girls put out.

He was ashamed of the thought even as it intrigued him. Brenna was a baaaaad girl. The worst. A criminal, a felon. Those reminders did nothing to lessen his desire.

Her makeup was dramatic, too—shimmering blue eye shadow, dark liner, shiny red lips.

He was in so much trouble.

"Okay, I'm ready," she announced as she slid her feet into her spike-heeled sandals. "We should take a picture and send it to Sonya. She was always a bit disdainful of my grunge look."

"She would be impressed," he said, and he thought he sounded pretty smooth, like one of those guys who routinely compliment any woman under seventy within their radar. Except Heath wasn't one of those guys, and he was afraid the slight catch in his voice gave him away.

"Oh. Uh, thanks." She looked away, and he thought she might actually be blushing. Was that possible? Or was she so *un*attracted to him that his compliment made her uncomfortable? Why was he suddenly asking himself all these questions? He wasn't normally so unsure of himself around the opposite sex.

"Hey, let's look at my guidebook and pick out all the must-sees," she said. "I don't want to miss anything."

Heath sat next to Brenna on her bed and peered over her shoulder as she thumbed through her travel guide, folding down page corners and circling the things that interested her. She made a lot of folds and circles.

"We won't have time to do all this stuff," Heath said.

"Don't be a wet blanket. The night is young. We'll do as much as we can do."

"And I suppose I'll have to pay for it all. I can't exactly put—" he read the attraction she'd just circled "—Queen LaDou's House of Voodoo on my expense report." He brought up money on purpose, to see how she would react.

"You don't have to pay for it all. I told you, I've got some cash."

"I thought Marvin wiped you out."

"I told you, Cindy gave me some money. Now, let's go. We'll start with dinner at House of Blues. Maybe this early there won't be a lineup."

UNFORTUNATELY THERE WAS a line to get in to House of Blues, but Brenna didn't mind so much. She felt a certain freedom, now that she'd decided to give up on finding Marvin. She could go back home, pick up the strands of her life and start living again. As for the company, she was more intrigued than ever with her stodgy FBI agent, who was not really so stodgy after all. Certainly a stodgy man wouldn't wear that shirt.

A waitress came by while they were standing in line and offered them beer. To her surprise, Heath bought them both a Beck's. She was touched he remembered the brand of beer she favored and a little surprised he wanted to imbibe.

"I *am* off duty," he said, chanting it almost like a mantra, as if he were trying to convince himself.

At least he talked in more than monosyllables. He asked

Brenna questions about her jewelry business, how she'd become interested in it, the process involved in making the type of jewelry she created.

Always excited to find someone interested in her passion, she'd told him everything he wanted to know—probably too much, she realized as she polished off her beer. The alcohol had loosened her tongue. Gawd, she'd probably bored the poor man silly.

"How did you get interested in law enforcement?" she countered.

"The same way a lot of people do—my father was a cop."

"You must admire him."

"I did. He's gone now."

"Oh, I'm sorry. Recently?" she asked, feeling genuine compassion. As badly as she got along with her parents, she still loved them and felt fortunate she still had them both.

"No, it was a long time ago." He smiled. "Let's not get maudlin. Tell me about your family. You mentioned parents. What about siblings?"

"A whole slew of them." She told him about her ultra-respectable brothers and sisters, and how she'd always striven to measure up—and failed.

"It's not like you're some vagrant living on the street," he said. "You have your own business. Isn't that a good thing?"

"Being a doctor or lawyer or accountant is a good thing," Brenna clarified. "Marrying one of the above is likewise good. Living in the Park Cities and having one-point-two children is good. Living in a cruddy downtown loft, being single, working as an artist—bad."

"Your parents have obviously never seen bad."

His approval, though mild, warmed her from the inside out. Or maybe it was the beer. "You know what? I didn't like you when we first met. You were kind of cold and suspicious. But you're not so bad."

"Gee, thanks."

"No, really. The truth is, I don't get along with most people."

He looked startled by that assessment. "You're kidding. You get along with everyone."

"I don't. I'm shy."

He burst out laughing at that one. "Shy? You're about as shy as a pit bull puppy."

She sat up straighter. "I think you just called me a dog."

"I meant it in the nicest way. You're bouncy and friendly, but when you get something in your teeth you won't let go."

She pondered that description of her. "I'm shy," she insisted. "An introverted artistic type."

He looked her up and down, focusing a long time on her bare legs, then her cleavage, then finally on her eyes. "Is that why you try so hard to blend in?"

"I'm compensating," she said, deadly serious. "My parents sent me to therapy because they were *sure* something was desperately wrong with me, so I know what I'm talking about. I draw attention to myself because it's the only way I'll get noticed. Sometimes I push people away so they won't have an opportunity to push me away first."

"My God, you're serious."

"You don't have to look so stricken. I'm cool with how I am. I deal with my shortcomings in unconventional ways, but they work for me. How about you, ever been to therapy?"

He didn't answer, because they'd reached the head of

the line and a hostess seated them. When he spoke again, he changed the subject to what was on the menu.

Okay, I got too personal. Heath's more relaxed manner had lulled her into thinking it was safe to reveal things about herself, and to expect he might reciprocate. Wrong. She was doing everything wrong where Heath was concerned.

Brenna chose something relatively bland, in deference to her still-quirky stomach. The live music was loud enough that they didn't have to talk much, giving Brenna a chance to regroup.

She shouldn't even care what Heath thought of her. It had only been a few weeks since things had ended so badly with Seneca—*Marvin,* she reminded herself. She'd thought herself totally in love with him, and discovering he was a complete phony had been devastating to her already-fragile self-esteem.

She had no business even *thinking* about getting involved with someone else, especially someone so wrong for her, even if he was eminently touchable, seeming more delicious by the moment. She'd long ago given up one-night stands, once she'd figured out that wasn't the way to a man's heart. Just because she was feeling a tad stupid and unloved was no reason to throw herself at the nearest cute guy.

With her self-control firmly in place, they left House of Blues and proceeded to seek out all the attractions in Brenna's guidebook. They visited a voodoo museum, which wasn't nearly as spooky as Brenna had hoped. It was all rather hokey and touristy. Against Heath's better judgment they went to a cemetery, which was known to be haunted not by ghosts, but by violent gangs.

"You're a cop," Brenna argued. "You've got a gun."

"Yeah, and I'm just dying to use it on some drugged-up kid."

However, Brenna convinced him they would be safe enough if they stayed within sight of one of the many organized tours that frequented the cemetery. Using her map, they located some of the more notorious tombs, including one of the purported final resting places of voodoo queen Marie Lavou. Previous visitors had left offerings—flowers, herbs and, to Brenna's disgust, a dead frog.

She shivered. "Maybe we should have brought Marie an offering," she said as she dragged Heath away from the creepy crypt.

As they walked past a tomb overgrown with weeds and vines, a startled bird burst out and flew right past Brenna's face. She shrieked and grabbed on to Heath's arm in an instinctual move. He laughed and put his arm around her. "Let's get out of here."

They wandered Bourbon Street for a while, amazed by the array of strange-looking people, most of them loud and drunk. Brenna didn't even draw a second look in this environment, and for once she was happy to blend in.

They stumbled across the famous Preservation Hall, an unimpressive barn of a room with crowded wooden benches for the patrons. A group of elderly black musicians blasted the room with raucous Dixieland jazz. Heath and Brenna managed to find an empty spot on one of the benches when another couple vacated it. But it was a tight squeeze and they were forced to sit very close.

Well, "forced" wasn't exactly the word Brenna would have used. She enjoyed feeling Heath's hips and the length of one thigh pressed up against her. The music wove a spell of timelessness around them. She was struck by the strange ambiance of this place, by the fact that if they'd visited ten years ago or thirty or fifty years ago, it probably would have looked and sounded just the same.

When the band took a break, they reluctantly gave up their seats, but only because Brenna had lots more things she wanted to do.

"What's next?" Heath asked affably, seemingly content to let her lead the way.

"A he-she revue."

"You mean—oh, no, I'm not going into one of those places."

"Oh, come on, it'll be educational. Unless…" Brenna gasped melodramatically. "You're worried you'll find the dancers attractive." She was only kidding. If she'd ever met a man who was secure in his resolutely hetero status, Heath Packer was it. "Come on," she wheedled. "Just five minutes. Just so I can say I've been."

He sighed. "All right. But you're paying the cover charge."

She did, happily. It was exorbitant, but it included a free drink. She got them each a watered-down beer. Heath sat and stared at the floor. Brenna watched the dancers, fascinated.

"I can't believe she's a man," she hissed at Heath. "I think it's fake."

Heath glanced at the stage impassively. "*She* has an Adam's apple," he pointed out. "And look at the hands."

The dancer did, in fact, have large, masculine hands.

Brenna watched for about another thirty seconds, before the stripper had taken off too many clothes. "Okay, I'm ready to leave."

"Thank God." They left most of the unappetizing beer behind. Once they gained the relative safety of the street, Brenna burst out laughing. "You were turned on."

"Was not."

"Were to."

"If I'm turned on, it's because of you, not some tricked-out guy."

A charged silence surrounded them. Then Heath seemed to realize what he'd said. He opened his mouth again, as if to refute his previous statement, but no more words came out.

It took a while, but Brenna found her voice. "Well, good." Then she headed down the sidewalk, feeling inordinately pleased. So, he wasn't immune to her. Even if she had no intention of following up, it didn't hurt her pride any that he found her attractive.

They ended up at the famous Pat O'Brien's courtyard, where Brenna insisted they each try one of the bar's signature drinks, a Hurricane.

Heath took an experimental sip of the frozen pink cocktail, served in a tall, curved glass. "Hmm, not bad."

"Have you ever had one before?"

He shook his head. "Real guys don't order fruity drinks. They drink beer. Or Scotch." He punctuated that observation with a manly growl.

"Oh, please." Brenna tasted her own drink. It was very sweet, and if it had any alcohol at all in it, she couldn't taste it. But she was hot and thirsty from running around the French Quarter, so she drank it. "These things are supposed to be really potent."

He took another sip. "I don't think so. It's tasty, though."

Just then a bright flash temporarily blinded Brenna. When the spots quit dancing in front of her eyes, she saw that a photographer had caught them on film.

"Hey, Packer!" Heath looked up, startled, as Grif Hodges approached them. "I thought that was you. Mind if we join you?" Grif had a very young, very pretty girl on his arm who stared up at him adoringly, hardly able to tear her gaze away long enough for introductions.

"Pull up a chair," Brenna said, noting Heath's tepid smile. Was he wishing he could be alone with her? Surely not.

Brenna struck up a conversation with Grif's date, Melissa, while the men put their heads together and earnestly discussed something in low voices.

"Cop talk," Melissa said, clearly intrigued. "What do you suppose they're discussing?"

Brenna shrugged.

"Have you and Heath been together long?"

"Oh, we're not together. Exactly." Brenna giggled, then looked at her drink suspiciously. She wasn't usually a giggler. Then she found herself telling Melissa the story of chasing after Marvin Carter.

"You're not giving up, are you?"

"We don't have any more leads. Anyway, I've got to get home and get back to work. My rent's due and I don't have any way to pay it."

"That's really an awful story," Melissa said. Then she nudged her date. "Grif, catch that waitress and order another round."

Despite the fact that Brenna and Heath both protested, they each ended up with another Hurricane. Brenna, who was feeling a buzz after only half of the previous one, left hers untouched. Heath, however, had drained his and immediately went to work on the second.

Brenna leaned over and whispered in his ear. "Be careful. I think these Hurricanes are stronger than we thought."

He looked at her quizzically. "Really? I don't feel anything."

She shrugged. Maybe Heath had a high tolerance for alcohol.

Brenna and Melissa chatted easily a few more minutes when Brenna felt a hand on her knee. She looked over, startled, to see Heath still trading cop stories with Grif. But that was unmistakably Heath's hand on her knee. Now it was rubbing sensually against the skin of her inner thigh.

"You okay?" Melissa asked. "You look like you swallowed a bug."

"Oh, no, I'm fine. Yesterday I had a touch of food poisoning," she said, grossly understating the situation. "I'm just not quite myself."

Melissa made sympathetic noises, and Heath looked over, as if his radar had just picked up something interesting. "Are you feeling okay, Brenna?" He removed his hand.

"No, I'm okay, really. Really." She wanted that hand back on her leg more than she could say.

He checked his watch. "It's late, and I've got a long drive ahead of me tomorrow. Maybe we should call it a night."

Brenna wanted to protest. She was having fun. She told herself it was because she'd missed Sonya and Cindy's female companionship, and she was enjoying Melissa. But it was Heath's attention that got to her. If she thought for even one minute he wanted to get her alone, she would leave in a heartbeat. But now he was all concerned about her health and getting a good night's sleep. As soon as they started walking, he would lose the intimacy they'd found and that would be it.

She opened her mouth to object again, but Heath was already standing, throwing bills onto the table for their waitress.

She'd lost her chance.

"Feel better," Grif said with a laugh.

As they left O'Brien's, the photographer tried to sell Heath the photo he'd taken of them. Heath shook his head, but Brenna whipped out some cash and paid the man. She clutched the photo as if it were the Rosetta Stone. She wanted to remember tonight. It had somehow become very important.

AS THEY HEADED BACK across the Quarter toward the Magnolia Guest House, a cool breeze kicked up, and for the first time since Heath had arrived in New Orleans, he was cold. He imagined Brenna, in her skimpy dress, was even colder. He put his arm around her.

"You okay?"

"I told you before, I'm fine."

"Good." In a weird, time-warp sort of delayed reaction, he realized he had his arm around her, that he'd kept his arm around her, and that it felt really, really good. And she'd put her arm around him, sliding it under his jacket, hooking one thumb in his belt loop.

"So what was all that knee squeezing about?" she asked.

"What?"

"You were squeezing my knee at O'Brien's. And feeling up my thigh."

"I didn't actually…" But if he'd only been thinking about putting his hand on her silky-smooth leg, how would she have known about it?

It was the Hurricanes. Come to think of it, the scene before him—the crowds of people meandering down Bourbon Street, the garish neon lights, the smells of booze and spicy Cajun food—had adopted a sort of movie quality, as if he was watching them on a screen, but not really there.

Or that he was acting a part, living in someone else's skin. And whoever that someone was, he wanted to take Brenna to bed with him.

As they gradually made their way out of the Quarter, the crowds thinned, the lights weren't so bright. Heath's steps slowed. The street seemed a suddenly treacherous place, not flat anymore but tilting dangerously first to the right, then to the left. He stopped and leaned against a lamppost.

"Heath?"

He pulled her around until she was facing him and put both arms around her shoulders. She was such a little thing. The top of her head barely came to his chin. "I think I might be drunk."

She grinned up at him. "I think you might be right."

"You did try to warn me."

"At least you can't accuse me of getting you drunk on purpose so I could have my wicked way with you." She put first one, then the other arm around his neck. "I think I like you tipsy. You're not quite so…rigid."

"Oh, I'm rigid, all right." The alcohol might have inhibited his customary caution, but it hadn't interfered with his libido. He was hard as a baseball bat. And as close as Brenna was leaning to him, she couldn't miss the fact.

"Are you going to do anything about it?"

"About being drunk? I could sleep it off, I suppose."

"About being rigid."

"I guess that depends on you."

"In that case…" She stood up on tiptoes and planted a luscious, moist kiss on his lips.

That did it. He was through being good, and cautious, and circumspect. He was finished playing by the rules. Where had the rules gotten him, anyway? He'd been toeing the line for months now, and still his supervisor didn't trust him.

Well, forget it. Once news filtered back to Ketcher that he'd been out on the town with Brenna Thompson—and it would, if Grif was the gossiping type—Ketcher would assume the worst. If Heath was going to hang for the crime, he might as well be guilty of it.

Chapter Six

Heath wrapped his arms around Brenna and deepened the kiss, grinding his mouth into hers, invading her with his tongue. She didn't seem to mind. In fact, she'd wrapped one of her legs around his, bringing their hips in closer proximity until he could feel her heat, even through multiple layers of clothing.

He moved one hand down to cup her bottom. And when that wasn't enough, he slid his hand under that tiny dress to caress one bare cheek. One *bare* cheek—

"Brenna Thompson, are you running around without underwear?"

"It's a thong. I'm not a complete degenerate."

A very thorough exploration of her bottom told him she was wearing something, but not much. He wanted to see what it was. He wanted to know what color it was. He wanted to pull it down her legs.

"If this kiss gets any crazier we're going to get ourselves arrested," Brenna whispered into his ear.

"Then let's go someplace."

"How far to the hotel?"

"I don't know. A few blocks."

"I can't make it," she said, sounding desperate.

He was sober enough to know he couldn't make love to her in the street. Not even in New Orleans would they tolerate that sort of behavior, and he had no idea whom he would call to bail them out of jail.

"We can make it," he said, as if they were a couple of mountain climbers trying to crawl the last few feet to the top of Everest. He pulled her dress down, gave her bottom a little pat. "If we run."

"Run?"

Intense physical activity was the only thing that was going to prevent him from exploding like a teenager making out for the first time. He grabbed Brenna's hand and took off at a brisk trot.

"Hey, no fair, I'm wearing spike heels, you know!" But she was laughing hysterically, doing her best to keep up the pace he'd set.

After a couple of blocks, he stopped and looked around in every direction. No Grif. He had a sneaking suspicion they'd shaken off their babysitter.

"Do you think we're going the right direction?" he asked.

"I thought you knew where we were going!"

But somehow, through divine providence or blind luck, they found themselves in front of the Magnolia Guest House. They stopped on the walkway in front of the building, gasping and laughing, as Brenna pawed through her little purse.

"I can't find my key. I can't find my key!"

"I've got mine." But as he patted his pockets, he realized he might have left his keys in Brenna's room. When he'd seen her painting her toenails, he'd lost all sense.

This was ridiculous. Neither of them had a room key? "Hell, what do we need a room for?" Heath steered Brenna toward a low, cast-iron gate that led into a side court-yard. It was full of shadows and featured wide, stone benches hidden from view by low-hanging branches of the titular magnolia trees. He maneuvered her to the darkest, most private corner he could find, then gently took the purse and the photo out of her hands and laid them aside.

She looked around, apparently only now realizing what Heath had in mind. "Here?" she asked, looking surprised and delighted by his audacity.

In answer he pulled her against him and kissed her, this time soft and sensual, teasing her lips with his tongue as he pushed the stretchy dress off her shoulders. Her full breasts were contained only by the slightest wisp of a red bra. Heath made quick work of the front clasp, and then they were his, heavy and ripe and definitely all her. He buried his face in the cleft between them, then kissed first one, then the other, delighting in the feel of her nipples hardening against his tongue as he provoked them.

She made an impatient sound as she tugged at his belt. "Would you hurry up!" As she gave one particularly hard tug, he lost his balance and fell backward onto the stone bench, barely managing to catch himself before he tumbled all the way onto the ground and landed on his head.

They both laughed, then at the same moment realized how loud they were being and shushed each other. Brenna knelt on the bench with his legs between hers and yanked off his jacket. "Is that a gun in your holster, or are you happy to see me?" she said, thumping the actual gun—not his other weapon.

He could be cavalier about a lot of things, but not his gun. "Hold on." He removed the holster, then set it gently on the ground behind him. "Continue."

He enjoyed letting her undress him in her funny, frantic way. And when he was naked from the waist up, he took over, pushing off his khakis and underwear, socks and shoes all in one slightly uncoordinated movement. Then he crooked his finger at her. There was just enough ambient light that he could see her, and he assumed she could make him out, too.

"Have you ever had sex outdoors?" she asked as she unzipped her dress and stepped out of it. She was a vision in nothing but a red thong.

"Yes. You?"

"You have?" She sounded shocked.

He and Christine had made love *everywhere* early in their courtship, but he didn't want to think or talk about Christine. "Not now."

He reached out and hooked his fingers in the thin straps of her thong, then slowly peeled it off her. She shivered.

"Cold?"

She shook her head. "Just incredibly turned on."

He pulled her onto his lap, both of her legs to one side, and wrapped his arms around her. He nuzzled her neck and flicked his tongue into her ear. Then they were kissing again, and after a few moments he nudged her hips until she maneuvered herself into straddling him again. But this time there was nothing separating them.

Nothing. "Brenna, we can't…we don't have…"

"Check my purse." He did and amazingly found what he was looking for.

"I love a woman who's prepared," he said just before ripping open the foil packet and sheathing himself. Then his attention was back on Brenna.

He wondered if his heart could explode from beating too fast. She inched closer to his arousal, kissed him, skooched up a little more. He reached down and barely brushed the flower of her womanhood with one finger, and she rewarded him with a gasp of pleasure. She was warm and slippery wet…for him.

She leaned closer and nipped him on the neck, distracting him for a moment as she raised up on her knees slightly. Then she was on him, welcoming him inside her, enveloping him with her softly scented warmth.

He'd never felt anything like it. Nothing, not even his very early sexual explorations, could compare to the excitement Brenna's intimate embrace had built inside him—not just in his groin, where it was expected, but inside his head.

Maybe it was the Hurricanes, he thought again. Or maybe it was just Brenna. He'd been with generous lovers before—his ex-wife had always been willing. But he couldn't recall any woman being as uninhibited, as ravenous, as Brenna. Her hunger, her sheer unbridled enthusiasm, actually matched his.

He didn't think he would last long, especially when she started to move with him inside her, slowly riding his erection. He was so aware of every nuance of the places they touched—not just the obvious ones, but the feel of her oddly textured hair against his cheek, his neck, the light rake of her fingers, with their short, utilitarian nails, on his chest, that moist cherry of a mouth kissing his shoulder.

Their lovemaking was an exquisite dance, a living, breathing, mobile work of performance art, a symphony that built to an ear-splitting crescendo as he exploded inside her.

They both managed to muffle twin cries of ecstasy, then they both started laughing. Heath didn't find their lovemaking particularly funny—it was a physiological reaction to the release of tension combined with pure nerves.

He cupped her face and kissed her, not able to find any words to express how wonderful it had been. Anything he could have said would have sounded trite, would have lessened the moment. So he settled for the kiss. He felt moisture on his thumb and realized she was crying.

Her vulnerability endeared her to him even more. He hugged her, feeling a rush of affection for this funny, rambunctious woman who claimed to be shy.

They heard noises right outside the fence. Someone else was arriving back at the guest house. Brenna slid off Heath's lap, grabbed her discarded clothes, and withdrew behind the tree trunk to dress.

"Would you please hide yourself?" she hissed, though she was trying not to laugh.

He didn't think anyone would see them unless they were making an effort to peer into the courtyard, but he quickly pulled on his pants, anyway, tucking his briefs into one pocket. He put on his shirt, now missing a couple of buttons due to Brenna's energetic disrobing efforts.

Brenna started digging around in her purse again. "Oh, my gosh, it was here the whole time," she said, triumphantly holding up her key. Hand in hand, they exited the courtyard and ran up the exterior stairs, laughing like a couple of kids cutting school.

It took both of them to get the key into the lock. The door opened and they more or less fell into the room. As soon as the door closed, Brenna threw her arms around Heath again as if they hadn't just slaked their thirst in a thorough and satisfying manner.

"I think I want you again."

"Have a heart, missy. I'm not a superhero."

"I think you are." She kissed him, warm and wet and uninhibited.

They stepped and stumbled their way toward Brenna's bed. Some of their clothes found its way onto the floor, but they didn't get far into a second bout of lovemaking before they both fell asleep.

BRENNA AWOKE as the first tendrils of dawn wiggled through the room's front window. She gasped as she realized exactly where she was—and who she was with. She was naked except for a thong and—one shoe? How did she sleep all night wearing one shoe? Her body was pressed along its entire length against Heath Packer, wearing only the *Miami Vice* shirt, one button fastened, the rest missing or undone. He was still dead asleep, looking deliciously rumpled with his day-old beard and his hair sticking up in odd directions.

She sighed expansively and laid her head against his chest. Then she tried to remember exactly what had happened last night. She'd drunk half a Hurricane, but she hadn't thought it had affected her much. Still…

The images flickered back, like flashbacks in an old movie. Oh. Ohhhhh. She giggled. Gawd, when had she become a giggler? And Heath—good Lord. The man had shown no restraint at all. Whether it was alcohol or something else that had made him so amorous, she didn't know. She was just glad it had happened.

She rubbed his cheek gently, hoping to nudge him awake. His rate of breathing didn't change at all. Poor thing.

She decided not to try to wake him, even though she knew he wanted to get an early start for Dallas this morning. She needed to get on the road, too, but she wasn't looking forward to going home. Her life was a complete shambles back in Dallas. Here in this strangely insulated world they'd created, where the sights and smells and tastes were so different from what she was used to, it was easy for her to forget reality. She wasn't ready to return to it.

But maybe Dallas wouldn't be so bad, if she had someone to offer her help and encouragement, and maybe a shoulder to lean on occasionally, as she picked up the pieces of her life, put her pathetically tragic broken engagement behind her. She had no idea what Heath's ideas were regarding the future—hell, she'd never even come out and asked him if he was already involved with someone. Though if he was, he'd kept it quiet.

But she couldn't help thinking that he wouldn't make love with her just because she was there and she was willing. He didn't seem like a casual-sex kind of guy. He was obviously conscientious about his job, polite and respectful to women in general. Guys like that didn't have indiscriminate sex with every female who crossed their paths. She wanted to believe, with all her heart, that making love had meant something to him. Because it had meant something to her.

She snuggled closer, throwing a leg over his, pressing her cheek into his crisp chest hair. Even in sleep, his arms snaked around her and held her close. She would stay like this, she decided, for as long as it took for him to wake up.

HEATH CRACKED OPEN one eye and was simultaneously aware of two things. First, the bright sunlight pouring into the room cut through his head like a machete. Second, the softly scented woman pressed up against him was giving him a raging woody.

He considered the woman first, because that seemed to be his most urgent concern. He angled his head down and saw the white-blond hair and a cute, rounded bottom.

Brenna. He was in bed with Brenna Thompson. And by the looks of things, they'd done more than sleep.

His chest swelled with an unaccustomed pleasure at the realization that Brenna's feisty flirtations hadn't been entirely for show—that she'd been attracted to him. But that momentary rush of pleasure was quickly replaced by darker, more disturbing realizations. Like, he didn't remember going to bed with her.

He struggled to get his uncooperative brain in hand even as he tried to corral his runaway libido. What, exactly, did he remember?

Going out on the town for their farewell evening in New Orleans. Dinner at the House of Blues. The voodoo museum. The cemetery. The he-she revue, he recalled, wondering how he'd let Brenna talk him into that one. Preservation Hall.

Yes, that part was all coming back to him. But then it started to get fuzzy…

Something was jabbing him in the shoulder. He lifted up slightly to find a cardboard folder of some sort with shamrocks all over it. Careful not to jar Brenna—because God knew he didn't want to face her until he'd figured out what had happened—he picked up the folder and opened it.

Inside was a black-and-white photo of himself and Brenna, sitting at a table on a patio with enormous drinks in front of them. They had their heads bent together, sharing a conspiratorial smile, looking for all the world like lovers.

The elusive memories fluttered just out of range like perverse butterflies. The folder was from Pat O'Brien's. The drinks—Hurricanes. They'd tasted like fruit punch, and he'd drunk two of them as if they were water.

Brenna had warned him, he recalled now. But he'd never been one to get easily drunk. He had enough body mass to absorb a helluva lot of liquor, not that he'd ever been much of a drinker. A beer or two occasionally while watching a hockey game, maybe a glass of wine with dinner...

Clearly he'd broken that pattern last night. His head was about to split open, his mouth felt like it was full of cotton, and his stomach was in not too good shape, either.

Brenna stirred. What the hell was he going to say to her? Good morning, I hope last night was good for you, because I don't remember a single moment of it?

He had to remember. How could he forget even an instant of making love with a woman like Brenna Thompson? He might have been the victim of temporary insanity, but if so, he should at least remember it.

Brenna stirred slightly. He needed to get out of this bed before she woke up. If he was really, really lucky, she wouldn't remember what had happened last night, either, and he'd be off the hook.

Moving an inch at a time, he managed to extricate himself from Brenna's tenacious but sleepy embrace. Now, if he could just find his clothes.

He spied his pants, crumpled on the floor where he'd left them. It worried him that he couldn't find any underwear. But when he stepped into the pants, he felt a bulge in his pocket and found his blue briefs. Now, that was damned odd. What were they doing there?

He panicked a moment when he couldn't find his gun and shoulder holster, but a quick search turned them up in the nightstand. At least, whatever inebriated condition he'd been in last night, he'd had enough presence of mind to take care of his Smith & Wesson.

He rebuttoned his shirt, noting the missing buttons—what in the hell had gone on last night?

He grabbed his jacket, stepped into his shoes, found his keys lying on the dresser, and tiptoed out of Brenna's room.

His room was two doors down by way of the balcony. He paused to take some slow, deep breaths, surveying the lush greenery and the birds flitting about in a side courtyard.

Something about that courtyard… He stared hard at it, willing himself to remember.

And then he did. The memories came rushing back to him like an out-of-control freight train, white-hot images of himself with Brenna in that courtyard, ripping off clothes, going at each other with hedonistic abandon.

He staggered from the shock of it. He'd made love in a public courtyard. With a suspect. With a woman he was going to have to arrest.

What had he been thinking? Just what the hell had been wrong with him that he would do something so stupid?

But the answer to that was easy. Nothing was wrong with him that wouldn't be wrong with any red-blooded male who'd spent the evening with Brenna in a tight red minidress. She'd been irresistible. All it had taken was enough alcohol to loosen his normally rigid control slightly, and he'd been a goner.

He didn't think Ketcher would be sympathetic with that excuse. He wondered if his FBI career was over.

"Hey." He jumped. Grif Hodges was coming up the stairs, looking way too chipper. "Have fun last night?"

"Did you?" Heath countered. "Was Melissa suitably impressed with your FBI macho-ness?"

"Ohhhh, yeah. She was dying to meet an actual crime

suspect, so I obliged her. But for the record, she liked Brenna and doesn't think there's any way Brenna's an art thief."

Heath groaned. "I don't, either. But I'm still stuck arresting her."

"That's what I'm here for," Grif said, almost cheerfully. "I'm supposed to escort you to the state line. You can handle it from there, right? Unless she gets really violent or something. You don't think she will, do you?"

"I don't know what she'll do." But he wouldn't blame her if she became positively homicidal when the man she'd made love with last night slapped handcuffs on her this morning.

WHEN BRENNA AWOKE a second time, it was to the crushing reality that she was alone in her bed. She sat up, rubbed her face, then wanted to kick herself for waiting to wake up Heath. They could have spent a leisurely morning in bed curing their hangovers with more sex. Instead, she'd fallen back asleep and Heath had no doubt awakened and made his escape before any awkward morning-after rituals could take place.

She looked around the room and saw no trace of Heath at all. No clothing left behind.

Had he been here at all? Or had she dreamed the whole crazy encounter? She knew that half Hurricane had given her a buzz, but it hadn't been enough liquor for her to manufacture an elaborate sexual delusion.

She picked up the pillow where Heath's head had lain and took a good sniff. Ah, yes. He'd been here after all. The scent of him was permanently embedded in her brain; she would know it anywhere, for the rest of her life, she imagined.

All right, maybe the fact that Heath had disappeared wasn't the disaster she'd thought. Some people were a little shy after a first sleepover, and Heath could be one of those, as reserved as he normally was. He might even be a bit uncertain how she would receive him, imagining that she'd seen him as some sort of drunken brute last night, ravishing her in a garden.

He might have gone out to get coffee and doughnuts and a paper, like yesterday. She soothed herself with those thoughts as she showered and brushed her teeth.

She had to really hunt for something presentable to wear, because she hadn't done laundry in a while. But she found her last pair of clean jeans, her most snug, faded pair, and a plain black T-shirt. She downplayed her makeup and combed the spikes out of her hair, letting it fall into a more natural, tousled look. She didn't want it to look like she was trying too hard.

She packed her suitcase. Still no Heath. Where was he?

She made one final check of the room, set her suitcase and purse by the door. Then, at loose ends, she decided to call Sonya.

Sonya answered on the first ring.

"Oh, my gosh, Brenna, I should have called you. Things have been so crazy here—"

"Stop, stop!" Brenna said on a laugh. "I didn't call to send you off on a guilt trip. How is your mom?"

"Holding her own. Well enough to be giving orders from her hospital bed and complaining about the food. Any sign of Marvin?"

Brenna quickly filled her in on the goings-on at the jewelry show and the elusive Alice/Ardith.

"So you actually found one of your pieces! How is it that she got away from you?"

That led to an explanation about Brenna's food poisoning.

"So he actually spent the night in your room taking care of you? I'm having a hard time picturing that. He seemed sort of—distant."

Not once you get to know him, she thought warmly. She didn't tell Sonya the most intimate stuff. Some things she had to keep to herself awhile longer, though she knew Sonya would be horrified and titillated all at the same time. Sonya put on a good show of being a straitlaced lady, but Brenna sensed a wild, uninhibited streak beneath her friend's polished exterior. "So how's the bodyguard?"

"Who? Oh, you mean John-Michael?" she said with a casual detachment that didn't fool Brenna for five seconds. "Annoying as usual."

"You've got the hots for him."

"What are you talking about? That's the most ridiculous thing I ever heard."

"Methinks the lady doth—"

"Oh, stop it. He's a boor, a complete heathen. A caveman."

"Cavemen aren't all bad."

There was a long pause. "I'll tell you about it sometime."

Brenna made her promise to fill her in when they both had more time. "And I want details."

After the phone call, Brenna felt terribly lonely. She wished Heath hadn't disappeared. Hell, she should just go find him. Maybe he'd fallen back asleep in his own room.

She stepped outside, taking a deep breath of the fragrant air. Somewhere close by, someone was baking. The smell of fresh bread made her stomach grumble. At least it was cooler outside, more appropriate for November. The uncomfortable mugginess was gone.

A door at the other end of the balcony rattled, then opened, and Heath stepped out. Brenna's heart swelled with unexpected emotion as she took in his tall, wide-shouldered body, neatly attired once again in a suit with a pressed white dress shirt. His armor, she thought with a grin. The suit was his protection against the world, his camouflage, so that no one saw what a funny and deeply passionate man he was.

He wheeled his suitcase out onto the balcony and closed his door before he spotted her. She smiled, feeling suddenly shy. She hadn't been kidding when she'd characterized herself as introverted. She'd learned to cope in different ways, so that she wasn't paralyzed in social situations or completely tongue-tied when meeting someone new. But at times, completely without warning, that shy little girl who stood in the shadow of her accomplished older siblings came to the surface.

"You're up," he said, clearly as ill at ease as she was.

"I've been up for some time. You…you didn't have to sneak out of my room this morning like a guilty thief."

He wouldn't meet her gaze. "Oh, yeah, I did."

"You think we did something wrong?"

"To put it mildly." His words were like spears tossed at her heart. She knew he was a bit more reserved than her, more conservative, but she'd thought what they shared last night, crazy as it was, had been special enough to transcend those little twinges of conscience Heath might be feeling.

"So it was, like, just a one-night stand for you? Is that it?" She struggled to keep her voice from going shrill.

"That's not it at all." He lowered his voice. "We were drunk."

"You might have been drunk, but I wasn't. I knew exactly what I was doing. And I thought you did, too."

"I might have known what I was doing, but it showed a remarkable lapse of judgment."

"You're not married, are you?" she asked, horrified at the possibility.

"No."

"Girlfriend?"

"No."

"Then what, exactly, is so objectionable?"

He didn't answer right away. That's when she realized she'd gotten it so, so wrong. He did sleep with her because she was convenient. And he had no desire, and no intention, to continue any sort of relationship with her. He was tossing her aside like yesterday's newspaper.

"I really thought better of you," she said in a small voice. "Not only that, I thought better of myself. I showed appalling judgment getting involved with Marvin, but I thought I was doing better with you."

"Under other circumstances—"

"Oh, don't bother," she said harshly. She opened her door and pulled her bag and purse outside. "No tender goodbyes, please."

"I didn't mean to—"

But she wasn't listening. She had to get out of there before she did something really humiliating, like cry. She couldn't do anything right. She couldn't even have a one-night stand correctly.

She wrestled her bag down the stairs, only to hear the *thud-thud* of Heath's shoes descending behind her.

"Let me—"

"I can do it." She started across the parking lot for her Honda, but Heath's hand closed around the suitcase's handle, stopping her.

"I can't let you go. I want to, believe me. But I can't."

She stopped, breathing hard. "What are you saying?"

"I'm saying I have to arrest you now."

Chapter Seven

Brenna's head started spinning, maybe from the vestiges of her hangover, but probably from shock. "Excuse me?"

"I have to take you into custody. We'll drive back to Dallas together."

Was he kidding? But she could tell by his grave expression that he wasn't. He was seriously going to arrest her.

"Might I ask what it is you think I've done?"

"Your parents turned you in."

This conversation was like a Fellini movie, all full of non sequiturs and symbolism so heavy no normal person could wade through it.

"I don't suppose you'd like to have this conversation over breakfast?" she asked. "Maybe start from the beginning so I can figure out what the *hell* you're talking about?"

"I don't want to have this conversation at all."

"So we're going to spend eight hours in a car without talking?"

"Unless you'd care to confess."

"Confess to what?"

He sighed, as if she were a truant schoolgirl who refused to mend her ways. Instead of answering her question, he pulled a pair of handcuffs from his pocket and gave her a look, like, *You're not going to make this difficult, are you?* Then she saw Grif Hodges leaning against a blue Jeep a few feet away, looking uneasy.

Now she knew why he'd seemed familiar. She'd seen him here, in the parking lot, in that Jeep. She'd been under surveillance the whole time.

With her spine straight, she put her arms in front of her.

Heath cuffed one, then gently twirled her around and fastened the cuffs behind her. "Sorry, it's regulation," he said as he read her Miranda rights.

Heath felt sick to his stomach, and it wasn't just the mammoth hangover that caused his discomfort. He hated what he'd just done, what he yet had to do.

The unpleasant task was made a hundred times worse by what he'd done last night with her. He'd been not only stupid, but thoughtless and insensitive. He deserved everything he had coming his way. He deserved to lose his job.

He deserved Brenna's revulsion.

But Brenna didn't look repulsed or disgusted. As he put her in the backseat of his car, her hands cuffed behind her, what he saw in her eyes was pure hurt and bewilderment. She didn't just feel she'd been done wrong. She'd been betrayed.

He couldn't read her thoughts precisely, but he had a pretty good idea of what was going on inside her head. She felt stupid for opening up to him, for believing him when he'd said he was on her side, for trusting him with her body. If she was Marvin's victim, rather than his partner, it was a miracle she'd trusted anyone again, particularly so quickly. But he suspected that was Brenna's way.

He'd thought, the first time he met her, she was as open and forthright as a daisy, that there was nothing secretive about her, nothing held back. Of course, he'd mistrusted his impression. But now he was really starting to wonder if the evidence was lying—and Brenna telling the truth.

"How am I going to get my car back?" she asked, maybe because it was easier to focus on the mundane than the crux of the real problem.

"You'll have to arrange with someone to come get it."

"Because I'll be in jail."

"Once your bail is set, you can get out."

"How much will that be?"

"That's up to a judge." The judge might listen to what Heath had to say about the suspect, but Heath intended to stay out of it once he'd delivered her into the system. His job wasn't to figure out why people did what they did. His job was to bring them into custody and provide the evidence a U.S. attorney needed to put them in prison. Understanding motive helped, but it wasn't a necessary factor.

He slid behind the steering wheel, started the engine, adjusted the vents and the mirrors, and finally pulled away from the curb to start the beginning of what he knew would be a long, uncomfortable journey. Grif's Jeep followed.

After fifteen minutes of tense silence, Brenna finally deigned to speak to him. "I'm hungry."

That figured. Apparently nothing short of near-fatal food poisoning could blunt her appetite, not even being arrested.

"What would you like to eat?" he asked.

"Waffles, sausage, and fresh-squeezed orange juice. Oh, and about a gallon of coffee."

He ignored her unreasonable request and pulled into the drive-through lane of the first fast-food joint he saw.

"What if I have to go to the bathroom?"

"We'll cross that bridge when we come to it."

"We've come to it. I have to go. Now."

He sighed, pulled out of the drive-through lane, and into a parking place. Though he suspected she was manipulating him in the only way available to her, he couldn't very well say no. He didn't want to be accused of abusing a prisoner in custody. He got out, opened the back door, took her arm and helped her out.

"You mean I have to walk through the restaurant in cuffs?"

"It's regulation."

"Forget it. I don't have to go."

He put her back in the car, but first he redid her cuffs so her hands were in front. She couldn't ride eight hours in a car with her hands cuffed behind her, he reasoned. Anyway, she wouldn't escape. She would face the accusations against her head-on. He knew that about her as surely as he knew his own name.

"Could you at least tell me what it is you think I've done?" she asked, trying to sound reasonable. "You believe I'm in cahoots with Marvin? That I helped him rip off Sonya and Cindy, then I helped him get away?"

"We'll talk about it later." In truth, he didn't want to talk about the charges against her at all. She would be formally interrogated once she was processed in Dallas, probably not by him, since Ketcher already believed Heath was too soft on Brenna.

"This is worse than the car trips I used to take with my family," Brenna muttered as she unwrapped her sausage-egg sandwich a few minutes later. "We had a minivan, and I always had to sit in the middle in the backseat, because I was the shortest and my father didn't want his rear view blocked. I couldn't see out the windows, and the air-conditioning vent didn't blow on me at all."

Heath resisted commenting. He'd been an only child

himself, and the car trips that were a rite of passage for most middle-class kids were miserable for him, too, mostly because he never had any other kids to talk to. He didn't think Brenna would enjoy having him point out that she'd been lucky to travel with brothers and sisters.

For a long time they didn't talk. Heath somehow managed to successfully negotiate the freeways and get on I-10 toward Baton Rouge. He had to endure the odious smell of that greasy sausage, and twice he had to crack the window when he felt in danger of retching.

"How come you're not eating anything?" Brenna asked when she'd finished.

"Can't you guess?"

"You're hungover?"

"Given my condition last night, are you surprised?"

"I didn't think you were *that* drunk last night. A little bit happy, a little bit relaxed, maybe even tipsy. But—"

"Well, I was."

"Hmm. I don't think so. You had the presence of mind to remember birth control. Also, I've always heard drunk men can't, um, perform as well as you did."

He didn't want to have this conversation. He wanted to forget last night had ever happened, and he desperately wished Brenna would, too. He didn't suppose there was much chance of that. "You'll have to trust me on this. I was smashed."

"Because that's the only way you could possibly have gone to bed with me? If you'd been sane and sober, no way in hell?"

"Pretty much." When he realized how that sounded, he backpedaled in a hurry. "I mean, not that I didn't want to. You're very, um, pretty." Ouch, that was lame.

She made a disgusted noise from the backseat, indicating she agreed with him.

"You're a suspect," he tried again. "No matter what my personal feelings toward you were, I shouldn't have let it happen. I shouldn't have even been drinking, even if I did think it was fruit punch."

"Are you gonna get in trouble for it?" she asked, obviously relishing the idea.

"That depends on you."

"You don't actually think I'm going to keep quiet about it, do you?"

He sighed. "I'd hoped."

"I'm going to tell anybody who'll listen. I'll take out a full-page ad in the *Morning News*—no, better yet, a billboard on LBJ Freeway. Because I think what you did was the lowest of the low, worse than what Marvin did, even. At least Marvin had an agenda I can understand. He wanted to gain my trust so he could rip me off. All you wanted was a thrill. Did you think about putting the cuffs on me even while we were making love? Did that turn you on?"

"It wasn't like that."

"Well, I'm telling," she said again. "And I hope you lose your job."

"You'll probably get your wish."

BRENNA COULDN'T IMAGINE why she was wasting even a moment of guilt on Heath Packer. He was a lying, traitorous SOB who'd taken advantage of her vulnerable state. He'd tried to get her drunk by telling her the Hurricanes didn't have any liquor in them. He'd made love to her knowing full well that, almost before they got their clothes back on, he'd have to arrest her.

But the last thing he'd said to her, so quiet and resigned, had gotten under her skin. *You'll probably get your wish.*

Would he really lose his job? Though the idea held some appeal, she wouldn't really blab about their liaison. It was too embarrassing. But he had no way of knowing that.

Though she was reluctant to even speak to him, she needed to know a few things.

"I'd like to know what I'm being charged with."

"It's not really my job to discuss—"

"Tough. You owe me that much."

"If we have this conversation, I'll have to record it."

"Fine, do it. I have the right to remain silent, but that doesn't mean you have to, does it?"

After more attempts to weasel out of it, he finally did pull off the Interstate. Then he pulled out a small digital recorder from the glove box, wedged it between the passenger seat and the center armrest, and began.

"You'll be charged with conspiracy, aiding and abetting, also possibly interstate transportation of stolen art."

"Stolen art?"

Heath sighed. "Two works of art by Picasso. One is a small painting of a girl with a cat. The other is a drawing he did in preparation—"

"I'm familiar with the pieces in question. Are you saying those paintings were stolen?"

Their eyes met in the rearview mirror, and the message in his was crystal clear. *As if you didn't know.*

"Assume, for the moment, just for fun, that I have no clue what you're talking about," she said.

"Yes, your parents' home was burglarized while they slept. There was no sign of forced entry," he continued, as if reciting rules of grammar from an English book. "The only items taken were those pictures."

"And you think I did it because…"

"Your parents showed us the note," he said, as if admitting to her some terrible, painful truth. "I'm sure you thought they wouldn't," he added. "You probably thought they would be too embarrassed to admit to the police that their own daughter would steal from them. And if it would make you feel any better, they were very reluctant to show us the note. Your mother was in tears."

Note? Brenna's blood pounded in her ears. She racked her brain, thinking of some time she'd made reference in writing to the Picassos. But she couldn't recall anything like that. As an artist and a student of art she'd always admired the painting, of course. But there were many beautiful works of art in her parents' home, many she liked better than the Picassos. None quite as valuable, though.

"What note are you referring to?" she finally asked.

Again he caught her gaze in the rearview mirror. He seemed to be begging her to give up the pretense of innocence, to stop forcing him to continue with this sham.

"What note?" she repeated.

"The one you left pinned to the wall, where the painting used to be. It was sent to the lab, of course. It had your fingerprints all over it, and the handwriting was definitely yours."

This made no sense. Could fingerprint experts be wrong? What about the handwriting analysis? Was it that exact?

The only explanation she could come up with was that someone was giving Heath false information. But who? Who hated her enough to want to see her convicted of a theft?

"Someone, somewhere, is lying," she said, hating that her voice shook with the emotions she was trying desperately to keep under control.

"Are you saying your parents—"

"No, not them. We have our differences, but the worst thing they would wish on me is—I don't know. To marry an accountant. They don't want me in jail. That would only humiliate them."

"Brenna, I saw the note. I handled it myself, turned it in to the lab, talked personally with our fingerprint guy and the graphoanalyst. There is no question, none whatso- ever, that you wrote that note."

Brenna slumped back into her seat. Had she slipped into an alternate universe? Was she the victim of some cruel reality show?

"We also found the drawing in your apartment," he said softly, as if that clinched the deal.

"You've been in my loft?" was the only objection she could think to make. The day she and Sonya had taken off for Cottonwood, she'd left the place a complete wreck. Odd that when he was telling her an incriminating item of stolen property had been found in her home, the one thing she could find to feel embarrassed about was the fact Heath had seen that she wasn't a meticulous housekeeper.

Perhaps the other was so extreme, so beyond her reality realm, that she couldn't even consider it.

"Is there anything else?" she asked, wanting to hear the worst. Of course, there was no guarantee he was being honest with her. Their entire acquaintance had been based on a sham; she had no reason to believe he would tell her the truth now.

"There is the matter of the twelve thousand dollars cash you're carrying around in your suitcase."

"You looked in my suitcase? That's—that's an illegal search," she said indignantly. Oddly, she was more upset that he'd violated her privacy than the fact he'd found the money.

"You're right. I can't use what I found as evidence in court, anyway. But it did give me pause. Innocent people don't normally carry around wads of cash that could finance a small terrorist group."

"If you'd just asked, I could have explained."

"So explain now."

She contemplated remaining silent. How dare he! But her silence would only be construed as guilt, she reasoned. "Cindy recovered three hundred thousand dollars that was stolen from her. She knew Sonya and I were at the end of our financial ropes, so she gave us some money to continue the search for Marvin."

"You're telling me she just handed you twelve thousand dollars in cash? No one does that."

"You don't know Cindy. Money's not important to her. Why don't you just ask—oh, wait. She's in Italy on her honeymoon. But you could ask Sonya. She'll back up my story."

"I'll do that," Heath assured her. "But I thought Sonya was rich."

"Not after Marvin got done with her." There was no point talking to him, Brenna decided. He'd not only arrested her, he'd tried, convicted, sentenced and hung her. And to think she'd been starting to *feel* something for the lout, which only proved what she'd already known: she had lousy taste in men.

IT WAS THE MOST UNCOMFORTABLE road trip in history. Heath endured hour upon hour of Brenna's stony silence, her accusing eyes staring resolutely at him in the rearview mirror. Those eyes made it nearly impossible to drive. He could hardly sit still. He wanted to pull off the road, jump out of the car and run for his life. He'd never seen such naked emotion in a pair of eyes. But then, he didn't believe Brenna was good at suppressing or concealing her feelings.

As they approached the Texas-Louisiana border, Grif honked his horn, then pulled an audacious U-turn across the median. Heath wondered if he would cross Grif's path again, and whether Grif would manage to hold on to that cocky attitude. The Bureau had a way of putting miles on a man.

Not even lunch improved Brenna's mood. She ate her hamburger in silence, sucked down the chocolate shake he'd gotten for her and made particularly rude sounds with her straw when she got to the bottom, daring him with her eyes to object. But she never said a word.

After lunch they spent several more grueling hours without speaking. As they neared the Dallas city limits, however, he noticed a marked change in her behavior. She became fidgety, looking out the windows, her expression one of distress rather than anger.

"I want to see my parents," she declared suddenly.

"I'm sure they'll be in contact as soon as—"

"No, I don't want to wait. Take me to their house."

"I can't do that."

"I just need five minutes with them. You can be there the whole time, listen to everything. Hey, maybe I'll confess."

Somehow, he couldn't see that.

"I should be allowed to face my accusers," she tried again.

"You will. Just not now."

"I'll make a deal with you," she said, suddenly sounding very reasonable. "Give me five minutes with my parents, and I'll conveniently forget about last night. As far as anyone will hear from me, you were the soul of professionalism."

Oh, hell. She was cruel, really cruel. She had just given him the opportunity to wipe the slate clean—but only by doing something else that wasn't by the book. But maybe, just maybe, he could justify it. He could get the confrontation on tape—and maybe she would say something incriminating.

But would she keep her word? Would she really keep quiet about last night's indiscretion? Oddly, he believed she would.

"Take the Mockingbird exit to get to my parents' house," she said helpfully.

"I know how to get there." And just like that, he'd made yet another decision that was probably going to bite him in the butt.

Chapter Eight

Brenna knew that if she could just see her parents, she could straighten everything out. She felt a sense of renewed optimism as Heath drove the FBI-mobile down Beverly Drive and her parents' preposterously large house came into view. The house had made some sense when there were six kids living there. Now it was just her parents, but they wouldn't dream of downsizing.

"We're not going to live in some *condo*," Brenna's mother had said vehemently when Brenna had innocently asked why they continued to keep the house, with its expensive upkeep and astronomical Park Cities taxes. Brenna actually smiled at the memory of her mother's exaggerated outrage.

She persuaded Heath to remove her handcuffs for the meeting with her parents. Rubbing her chafed wrists with relief, she marched up to the front porch, Heath behind her with a discreet hand at her elbow. Out of habit Brenna punched in the security code. The alarm panel flashed red at her.

"They probably changed the access code, on our advice," Heath said mildly.

"In case I returned to steal something else?" She was beginning to feel as if she'd dropped down Alice's rabbit hole, because it was only in some alternate universe that her parents feared her entering their home unwelcome and stealing from them. She still couldn't believe they'd actually accused her, no matter what the freaking evidence said.

She rang the bell. She had a key somewhere in her purse, but if they'd changed the alarm access code, they'd probably changed the locks, too.

Annalisa, the Thompsons' live-in maid, answered the door. The moment she saw Brenna, her eyes lit up with surprise and delight, and she yanked Brenna inside and enveloped her in a welcoming hug.

"Brenna, I know you didn't do it," Annalisa said passionately in her softly accented English. And she gave Heath a menacing glare. "When those FBI people talked to me, I told them a thing or two."

"Thank you," Brenna said, not wanting to ever let Annalisa go. "Apparently they weren't listening, but thanks for trying. Are the folks home?"

"They're in the den watching *CSI*. They've taken a keen interest in crime shows since all this happened."

Annalisa led the way through the foyer, with its ostentatious crystal chandelier, into a huge room that was modestly called a den. It featured a dozen plush, reclining theater-style seats and a large-screen plasma TV, which was currently blasting *CSI* in surround sound. Brenna had taken all her family's trappings of wealth for granted when she'd been younger. It had seemed normal in her insulated world. It was only when she'd gotten out on her own that she'd realized how the rest of the world lived.

Her parents were in their favorite seats, the two in the middle of the front row, tumblers of some beverage tucked into their drink holders.

They both turned around when the door opened. Their faces froze in surprise at first. Then they were out of their seats and coming toward her. Her father muted the TV on the fly.

"Brenna, sweetheart, are you all right?" her mother asked.

Tears burned at the back of Brenna's eyes. She really hadn't been sure how she would be received, but the fact that her mother's first reaction was one of concern reassured her. She'd been right in coming here.

"I'm fine, Mom," she said, giving her a hug. It was less forceful than Annalisa's hug, a bit tentative. The Thompson family wasn't ordinarily a real touchy-feely bunch. "I'm so sorry if I worried you. I didn't realize anyone would notice or care if I took off on a lark."

"Normally we don't take that much notice when you behave strangely," her father said uneasily. "You've always been unpredictable."

"But…?" she prompted.

"Under the circumstances, of course we were worried."

"Can we all sit down?" Brenna asked. "Maybe in the living room?"

"Of course," her mother said, putting an arm around her in an uncharacteristically affectionate fashion. "Annalisa, could you fix us some drinks? Agent Packer, what would you like?" she asked with resolute politeness. Always be a good hostess, even to the man who was dragging your little girl off to jail.

"Nothing for me, thanks."

Brenna asked for a soft drink.

Her father led them into the more formal living room, with its Oriental carpets and silk-upholstered furniture. One glaring feature stood out the moment they entered the room—a huge blank space on the wall where the two Picassos had hung, side by side.

Before sitting down, Heath set his little tape recorder on the coffee table and switched it on. He did his usual thing—time, place, who was present.

"So, Agent Packer," her father said, taking command of the meeting as Brenna had known he would do. "Is my daughter under arrest?"

"Yes, I'm afraid she is," he said. "She made a request to speak to you before she's taken to headquarters and processed."

"Brenna," her father said urgently, glancing uneasily at the tape recorder, "I think we should call a lawyer before you say another word to anyone."

"There will be plenty of time for that," Brenna said, unconcerned. "I just need to hear it from you. Do you believe I stole those Picassos?"

Her parents exchanged uneasy glances.

"You can talk in front of Agent Packer," she said.

When her mother finally spoke, her voice was strained, as if she was fighting off tears. "We don't want to believe that any of our children would steal from us—steal from anyone. But we can't close our eyes to the facts."

"What facts?" Brenna urged.

"The note. It was your writing, Brenna. I don't need some fancy crime lab to tell me that. And it was the stationery I gave you for your birthday last year."

That was the part that didn't make sense. "I wish I could see that note," she murmured, almost to herself.

"I have a copy of it," her father said. His statement obviously surprised Heath, who sat up straighter. "I copied it before we called the police. I knew they would take it away as evidence, and, well, I just thought I might need it someday."

"Someday is now," Brenna said. "Dad, can you get the copy, please?"

"It's in my study." He disappeared just as Annalisa came in with the drinks, which she delivered efficiently. Brenna's mother took a bracing sip of her fresh cocktail, which was definitely Scotch. Francine Thompson hadn't been a Scotch drinker before. Brenna wondered what toll this situation was taking on her.

"Brenna," she said, setting the drink down. "Are you saying you didn't take those pictures?"

"Yes, that's exactly what I'm saying. Someone went to a great deal of trouble to make it look as if I did, but I didn't."

"But who would—oh." Her mother looked down. "Seneca." When she looked back at Brenna, her eyes were beseeching. "But he's so nice."

"He's not nice. He's not even Seneca. You know all those years you told me what dreadful taste I had in boyfriends? You were right. I'm not sure how much you've been told, but Seneca—Marvin Carter, actually—was engaged to two other women besides me, and he has since been working on at least two more."

Francine looked mortified. "I guess in retrospect, that long-haired guitar player with the tattoo wasn't so bad."

Heath looked at her questioningly.

"You don't want to know," Brenna said. Keith had been just another in her string of bad decisions where men were concerned.

Her father returned and handed her a piece of white paper that looked as if it had been much handled. She wondered how many times her parents had read it, trying to square it up with the daughter they thought they'd known.

Brenna started to read the note:

Dear Mom and Dad,
Let me say first that I love you, and I've never
stopped loving you—

She didn't need to read the rest. She laid the note on the
mahogany coffee table that sat between her and her parents. "I suspected it was something like this, but now I
know how it happened."

"Then you didn't write it?" her mother asked hopeful-
ly. Her father, she noticed, looked very uncomfortable. He
was obviously more convinced than his wife that Brenna
was guilty.

"I did write it," she said. "At Seneca's urging. We were
talking one night about why I didn't spend more time with
my family, and I told him how I just never fit in and how
everything I did felt wrong—"

"Oh, honey," her mother started, but Heath interrupted.
"Let her finish."

"Well, anyway, I explained to him about how Grandma
had died and left all that valuable jewelry to me, and how
everyone had been mad at me, like I'd somehow convinced
her to change her will or something. And that the gulf between us had just gotten so big I didn't know how to get
across it. And he suggested I write a letter. He said when
we try to put our feelings into words in person, we get emotional and embarrassed, and things get awkward. But he
thought if I could explain it on paper, just the way I'd explained it to him, that maybe it would...how did he put it?
Maybe it would *foster understanding* between us."

Francine nodded, her gaze locked on Brenna, hanging
on every word. Her father looked into his drink, but he was
listening intently, Brenna could tell.

And Heath—she was almost afraid to look, but she

made herself glance over at him. His eyes were fixed on her. He was utterly still, like a tiger scenting the air, trying to determine if what he smelled was predator, prey or maybe a potential mate.

She looked back at her mother. That was safer.

"Well, I tried to write that note," Brenna continued, "because I thought it sounded like a good idea at the time. But I made two or three efforts, and they all sounded lame, and I realized a letter where I poured out my feelings just wasn't my style. This was the last one. I got farther along, but still not very far. I crumpled it up and threw it away. Look, you can see the crease marks in the photocopy. I bet the original was wrinkled some, even if Seneca smoothed it out.

"The paper did have an odd quality about it," her father said. "As if it had been artificially stiffened somehow."

"It was probably ironed," Heath said. They all looked at him. "The lab found traces of spray starch on the paper. They thought it might be some part of the stationery manufacturing process."

The tightness in Brenna's stomach eased slightly. She took a sip of her Sprite. Marvin had been very, very clever. He'd retrieved the note from the trash and fashioned a crime around it.

"So that's why the note wasn't signed," Francine said. "It wasn't finished. The police said it was because you thought a note without a signature would be less incriminating."

"I'm not an idiot. My prints were all over the paper."

Heath leaned over and picked up the photocopy, scanning it. "But what did you mean by 'grand gesture'?" he asked. "If stealing valuable artworks wasn't the gesture, what was?"

Brenna felt embarrassed at having to admit her little scheme for getting back into the family's good graces, but she supposed she had no choice now.

"Grandma told me to take apart her old jewelry and melt down the gold and platinum. She wanted me to use the raw materials for my own creations. She was trying to help me succeed as a jewelry designer."

"You melted them down?" her father said, sounding distressed.

"Marcus, dear," Francine said, putting a soothing hand on her husband's arm. "Your mother had some extraordinarily ugly jewelry, even if it was valuable."

"My plan was to make a special piece for each member of the family. I was going to display them at the IJC show in New York. Remember I told you about that important show that I got accepted to?"

Her parents looked at her blankly. She'd told them, but it hadn't registered as important.

"Anyway," she continued doggedly, "after the show, I was going to give the new pieces to you all, as a peace offering. And I was going to explain that in the note, if I'd ever gotten that far. I just didn't want everybody mad at me anymore," she finished lamely.

A loaded silence descended. Did they believe her? she wondered. The story sounded ludicrous, even to her. Finally her mother spoke. "What were you making for me?"

Brenna smiled with relief. Her mother, at least, accepted the story at face value. "I hadn't actually made yours yet. You're the hardest, because you're so particular. But I saw something in New Orleans that gave me an idea—a dragonfly scarf pin with emeralds. Something really small and delicate."

"It sounds lovely." Francine usually dismissed Brenna's jewelry with a distracted, *Very nice, dear.* Brenna wasn't used to hearing such a heartfelt compliment. Then she realized her mother was crying.

"Mother?" Brenna didn't know what was wrong.

"I knew you couldn't have done it," she said.

Relief flooded over Brenna like Niagara Falls. Someone believed her. They both stood and managed to get around the coffee table without tripping. This time Francine's hug had some meat to it.

Her father cleared his throat. "There was no forced entry," he said, the single sentence throwing a pall over the room.

But Brenna could explain that one easily enough. "When I brought Seneca here to meet you, I used the code to get in. He was standing right there. He could have seen me punch it in and memorized it. And as for how that drawing got in my apartment, he put it there, probably immediately after the burglary. It only makes sense."

"He had a key to your apartment?" Francine asked, sounding slightly scandalized.

Brenna rolled her eyes. "Yes, Mom, he had a key."

"Well, there you have it," Francine said, addressing her comments to Heath. Then she turned to her husband. "Marcus, go call James Prince." James Prince was the family attorney specializing in tax law and estate planning. He'd probably never defended against a criminal charge more serious than a speeding ticket, but he would know whom to call.

"Mrs. Thompson," Heath said, "do you believe the story your daughter just told you?"

"Well, don't you?" When Heath hesitated, Francine charged ahead. "Agent Packer, I know my daughter. I didn't want to believe she'd stolen from me, but I couldn't come up with another explanation. But that's all changed now."

Brenna's throat tightened just knowing she had someone on her side.

"Most people don't want to believe that a family member—" Heath started, but Francine wouldn't let him continue on that thread.

"I'm not deluding myself," she said firmly. "Brenna's no angel, I know that. She's always had a tendency to take what she wanted." She paused, slightly flustered by what she'd just said. "What I mean is, she *went* for what she wanted, no holds barred, and sometimes she got herself into trouble. But one thing I know for certain is that she owns up to what she does. Agent Packer, Brenna is incapable of lying."

"I'm sure you—" Heath began again, but this time Marcus Thompson, in the middle of dialing someone on his cell phone, cut him off.

"Francine's right," he said. "Brenna might be capable of taking something that didn't belong to her, if she had a strong enough reason. But she would never lie about it. She couldn't. Everything is right there in her eyes to see. Always has been."

Francine nodded vigorously in agreement. "She couldn't tell a lie if her life depended on it. Not so anyone would believe her," she added. "If she says this Marvin person took the pictures and framed her for it, then that's exactly what happened."

Then both Brenna's parents stared at Heath, daring him to persist with his accusations. Brenna stared at him, too. She knew what he had to do. He was under orders to bring her in. Even if her parents dropped the complaint against her, she faced other charges. She was still suspected of aiding and abetting Marvin in his other crimes. But she wasn't going to make it easy on Heath.

He refused to meet their gazes—any of them. "We need to get going," he said gruffly. He reached for the tape recorder, turned it off and stuck it in his jacket pocket.

"You're still going to arrest her?" Francine screeched.

"I've already arrested her. It's not up to me to decide whether her story is credible or not."

"Can't we bail her out or something?" Marcus asked.

"Her bond hearing will be tomorrow. She'll have to spend the night in Lew Sterritt."

Brenna's heart sank. She'd held on to a shred of hope that she wouldn't actually have to spend any time in jail.

"Can't we speed things up?" Francine asked. "We know a judge or two."

Heath shook his head, looking more and more uncomfortable. "She has to be processed through the U.S. Marshals Office first. They're closed until tomorrow morning." He stood and said again, "We have to get going." He was apparently as anxious as she to get this ordeal over with, one way or another.

They left amidst hugs from Brenna's parents and cautions that she shouldn't say any more until the lawyer showed up. Then she and Heath were walking slowly toward the LeBaron.

Heath opened the back door. But before she could even climb inside, he closed it again. "Hell, I can't do this."

Brenna's breath caught in her throat.

"I'm not going to take you in," he said. "You didn't do it."

Chapter Nine

Brenna's smile was bright enough to light up the dusky November evening sky. "You believe me?"

"No one who witnessed that scene with your parents could think you were guilty of anything." He leaned against the car, seemingly oblivious to the chill breeze that blew from the north. Brenna hugged herself to keep from shivering. And to think, yesterday they were sweating in the New Orleans humidity.

"You have to take me in…don't you?"

"Yes. But I'm not going to. I can't be the one to…" He couldn't finish.

"If you don't, someone else will, won't they?"

He nodded, the gesture filled with hopeless resignation.

"Then I want you to do it. Some other agent who doesn't know me might be, you know, mean. Anyway, won't you get in trouble?"

Heath studied her from the corner of his eye as he pretended to gaze into the distance. This was a bit of a reversal. A few minutes ago she'd been spitting mad at him, wanting to make his life as difficult as possible. Now she was worried about his job?

"If I don't bring you in, I'll get fired. I was on thin ice as it was."

"Why?"

"A previous incident. Something that's unconnected to you." Except that he'd trusted a woman he shouldn't have, a woman he loved very much. The powers that be would think the same thing was going on now.

And maybe it was. Maybe his trust was misplaced. He had little faith in his instincts, which he'd once thought were infallible. He'd been as wrong as a man could get with Christine. But he'd wanted to believe that was a one-time event, his single, solitary blind spot. Could it be happening again?

If so, then he had no business in law enforcement.

"I'm freezing," Brenna said. "Can we get back in the car?"

"Sorry. I should have realized." But he opened the front passenger door. She gave him a brief, questioning look before climbing inside.

When he was behind the wheel and they were driving away from her parents' house, he was still considering his options.

"Just take me in," Brenna said. "Let's get it over with. A night in jail isn't going to kill me, and Dad will hire a good lawyer, and they'll get me out. And then we'll gather whatever proof we need to get the charges against me dropped and refocus the investigation where it should be—on Marvin."

"Where it should have been all along, apparently," he said. "When I first came to Cottonwood looking for you, Marvin Carter was not even a blip on my radar screen. You were the main focus."

"You mean even after Cindy's three hundred thousand was recovered, the FBI still wasn't taking the case seriously?"

"I'd never heard of Cindy *or* her three hundred thousand. That was a separate case, one that Agent Delacroix was not aggressively pursuing. We combined them later, after you pointed out the connection."

"Why me? Why was my case such a hot priority?"

"A stolen Picasso makes for good press," Heath said. "A pretty young woman thief is even better."

"So you prioritize your cases based on press potential," Brenna said indignantly, fiddling with the heater controls. "You know what burns me?"

"I imagine a lot of things do at this point," Heath said as he pulled south onto I-35 toward the FBI Field Office.

"I'm going to have to pull out of the IJC show. I won't have time to work on new pieces for the show if I'm busy trying to prove myself innocent of conspiring with an art thief."

Heath was starting to understand how very important that show was to Brenna. He compared it to making the first cut at the FBI Academy in Quantico. If she pulled out of the show, it was like washing out at the academy. There would be no second chances for her.

The miscarriage of justice that was about to take place would impact her career, possibly for the rest of her life, even if she was completely, totally exonerated later on.

Heath drove his car more and more slowly as he approached the FBI Dallas Field Office at One Justice Way. Finally, despite his dawdling, he pulled into an empty spot. His arms and legs felt like lead.

"I could let you escape," he said.

Brenna actually laughed. "I'm not cut out to be a fugitive. Come on, let's get it over with. And don't you think you should handcuff me again?"

"You're turning yourself in. The minute you realized there was an arrest warrant with your name on it, you came voluntarily. That's my story, and I'm sticking to it."

Heath led Brenna down a narrow corridor to the processing area. At this hour of the evening, they had the place to themselves, which was just as well. He didn't want anyone else witnessing Brenna's humiliation.

First he took her mug shot. She stuck her tongue out during his first attempt, and he wondered how she could maintain a sense of humor through all this. However, once she realized this process was painful for him, she straightened up.

He peeled the backing off the Polaroid prints. She looked really sad, he thought. Tragic and beautiful, her eyes deeply shadowed, her blond hair drooping from its usual perkiness.

"Can I see?" she asked.

He obliged her, and she gasped. "Oh, my God, those are horrible. You have to take them again. Let me put some makeup on, comb my hair…"

"Brenna, no one takes a pretty mug shot, okay?"

"But what if I end up on the Post Office wall someday? I will hold you personally responsible if every postal customer in the United States sees these pictures."

He could not bring himself to laugh.

"Come on, Heath." She punched him on the arm. "It's not as bad as all that. I'll have a story to tell my grandchildren. That is, if they don't keep me locked up during all of my remaining child-bearing years."

He attempted a smile, but he imagined it came out rather sickly.

Next he had to take her fingerprints—three different sets, for various purposes. The process was strangely intimate. He had to stand very close to Brenna, hold her hand as he rolled each finger over the ink pad, roll it again onto a card. He could smell her hair, feel her breath on his skin. Would this be the last time he touched her? The last time they would ever stand so close?

She was subdued as she wiped her fingers with a towelette. He'd seen lots of arrestees in his years. At some point during the booking process, it hit all of them—this wasn't a game, no one was going to jump out from a phone booth and save them.

He took her to an interview room and got her a cup of coffee, though she said she didn't want one. "I have a few things I need to do. You'll be okay for a few minutes?"

"I might not ever be okay again," she murmured.

The first thing he had to do was go to the National Crime Information Center computer and remove Brenna's name, now that her arrest warrant had been officially served and she was in custody. If he forgot this crucial step, there was a chance she could get arrested again after she was out on bond, which caused cases to be lost, lawsuits to be filed and agents to lose their jobs.

Brenna's name didn't come up the first time he typed it in. He tried several variations, but she didn't seem to be in the system. Which was ridiculous—he'd put her there himself. Something strange was going on.

He would have to ask Ketcher. He dreaded calling the Supervisory Special Agent. Ketcher would no doubt want to be in on the interrogation. He might even ban Heath from the interview room, once he learned Heath believed she was innocent. But he couldn't put the unpleasant task off any longer.

He dialed Ketcher's number at home.

"Oh, I guess you didn't hear," Ketcher said offhandedly when he got on the line. "The charges against Ms. Thompson have been dropped."

"Is that why she's not in NCIC?" Heath asked, astonished.

"Yeah. The SAC himself told me to bury the case. I'm guessing Brenna's parents no longer wish to pursue it. I think it's a crock, but there's nothing we can do."

"So I can just let her go? What about the other charges?"

"Under the circumstances, we've decided to drop all charges. Without her parents' cooperation, the case is much weaker. Personally, I think her parents should reimburse us for all the money we spent chasing her down. If they didn't want her arrested, why did they turn her in in the first place?"

"People change their minds," Heath said, scarcely believing the good news.

He returned to the interview room and found Brenna standing on her head in the corner.

"Brenna?"

She toppled over, then pushed herself up to her knees, giving him a rueful look. "I got bored. If I'd known you were gonna be gone forever, I'd have asked for a magazine or—what are you grinning about?"

He opened the door wider. "You're free to go."

She stared at him, uncomprehending.

"Seriously. All charges against you have been dropped."

"What happened?" Brenna asked.

"Your parents. They must be pretty heavy hitters. One call to the special agent in charge, and you're off the hook."

A slow smile spread across her face. "Oh, my God, I'm a free woman! And I was just starting to wonder what sort of food they serve in jail." Then she flew across the small room and threw her arms around his neck in an exuberant hug. "Thank you, Heath."

"For what?" But he returned her hug, totally enjoying the feel of her warm, curvy body against his. Minutes ago he'd thought he would never experience that again. "I didn't do anything."

"Thank you for believing in me. And for almost trashing your career for me. What if I'd fled?"

"I knew you wouldn't. You're not that difficult to figure out."

She looked troubled by his assessment. "Do I really just let everything hang out? I wish I was more mysterious. Like Sonya. Now there's a woman with secrets."

"I don't care for women with secrets." He'd certainly had his fill with Christine. "Come on, let's celebrate."

He might catch hell from Ketcher for getting drunk and sleeping with a suspect he was supposed to be surveilling. It all depended on whether Grif Hodges kept his mouth shut. But Heath didn't want to think about that now. One crisis averted—he would enjoy that while he could.

While Heath drove to the West End, a touristy area of converted warehouses near the Trinity River where they would have plenty of restaurant choices, Brenna called her parents.

"I'm free!" she announced. "All charges dropped. I don't know what you did, but—" Long pause. "Uh-huh… really? So you didn't withdraw your complaint or anything?" Another long pause. "Well, I guess maybe James Prince did some fast-talking."

After a bit more speculation, Brenna hung up. "You heard?"

"Yeah." And it made him uneasy. Federal charges didn't just get dropped for no reason.

"I don't care how it happened! I'm just happy it did. Oh, how about Tony Roma's?" she asked as the West End's neon lights came into view. "I could eat an entire barbecued cow."

Those words were music to his ears. Brenna was back to normal.

A few minutes later, while they waited for their barbecue to arrive, Heath made a toast with his cola.

"Here's to your success at the IJC show. Now you can focus on getting ready."

"Oh, God." A panicked look came over her face.

"What? I thought you'd be happy."

She reached across the table and squeezed his arm. "I am. But now I have to come up with something to show in New York. I have nothing!"

"You've got a few days."

"Not that many. I was planning to show about fifty different pieces. I had at least half of them done before Marvin wiped me out. I can't possibly—"

"Yes, you can."

"Even if I had the time, I don't have the money to buy the raw materials I need. Gold, silver, platinum, and then there are the precious stones."

"How much would you need?"

"Thousands of dollars. But I couldn't borrow it from my parents, if that's what you're thinking. They've already done so much."

"What about your mad money?"

"What, Cindy's money?" She sounded highly offended. "She gave me that to use for catching Marvin. I can't just go spending it on personal things."

"Then let me lend you the money."

Brenna's face froze. She stared at him as if she hadn't heard him right.

"I think you're talented," he continued. "I want to invest in your career. Figure out the bare minimum of pieces you'll need for the show and make up a shopping list. If I can afford to pay for it, I will."

"You're being awfully nice," she said suspiciously. "Is there a catch?"

"No catch. Let's just say I have some things to atone for."

"Ah. Guilt."

He looked down. "I'm entitled to it."

BRENNA MADE RAPID NOTATIONS on a series of paper napkins. First she made a list of the pieces she wanted to reproduce. Fifty would be good, but she could maybe get away with thirty. She had no trouble remembering the rings and bracelets and earrings that had been stolen. Each was like a child to her, especially the ones she'd made for her family. On some she recalled exactly how many grams of gold or silver had been required for the casting; others she guesstimated.

As for the stones, there was no way she could afford, or even locate, stones that would match the fabulous specimens she'd harvested from her grandmother's old jewelry. Grandpa Jeremy, who'd died before Brenna was born, had traveled the world collecting unusual and rare stones, which he had made into the gaudy pieces he'd given his wife.

Brenna would be forced to substitute inferior stones—maybe even semiprecious. Blue topaz could be substituted for aquamarine, garnet for ruby, green tourmaline for emerald. Her mind raced with possibilities. Maybe she could do it. Maybe she could make it work! For the first time in days, she felt optimistic about her future as a jewelry designer.

And every so often she sneaked a peek at Heath, sitting across the booth from her. He was watching her, studying her thoughtfully, apparently enjoying the sight of her losing herself in her new task.

A sudden, disconnected thought came to her out of the blue. "Is my picture posted on some wall at the FBI office? You know, maybe with darts sticking out of it?"

Heath smiled. "No."

"Rats. I thought I was infamous. If a person gets themselves wanted by the FBI, at least they could be infamous."

Now Heath laughed, and it changed his whole image. She had a strong feeling that laughing came naturally to him, but that he deliberately suppressed the inclination.

"That reminds me," he said. "I have something for you." He reached into his inside jacket pocket and pulled out her mug shots and fingerprint cards.

"For my scrapbook," she said with a grin. "Wait till I show these to my mom. She'll freak. Hey, maybe I could have them laminated and hang them from my rearview— Oh, shoot! My car!"

"I'll get Grif to pick it up. He'll store it at the impound lot until you have time to go get it."

"But how am I going to get around?"

Heath hesitated, then said, "I'll drive you."

"Don't you have a little thing called a job?"

"I'm due some vacation."

"Yeah, but do you really want to spend it ferrying me around? Wouldn't you rather be in Maui or someplace?"

He shrugged.

He must have a lot of guilt to atone for, she decided. But she wouldn't look a gift horse in the mouth. If she was going to be ready in time for the IJC show, she would take all the help she could get.

In truth, she wasn't ready to see the last of Special Agent Heath Packer. Maybe having sex with him had been a colossal mistake. Maybe she should swear off men for a while. But she still liked having Heath around.

"Are we friends?" she asked as they walked back to his car. Without a jacket, Brenna shivered in the keen wind. She'd never had a guy friend before. Not a close, good friend, anyway.

Heath slipped an arm around her, in a brotherly sort of way. "I like you, Brenna. I guess that makes us friends, if you'll have me."

"Yeah, but how good a friends? Is it a 'maybe we'll run into each other again some time' kind of friends? I know you didn't mean to have sex with me—"

"Brenna—"

"No, let me say it. I was available, I was needy. It was my fault. It shouldn't have happened. But I like you, too, so let's not let that one night make us all weird around each other."

"Okay. No weirdness. Promise. I'll take you home, then I'll come back tomorrow and we'll go shopping."

She would have to be satisfied with that, she supposed. At least he hadn't told her to flake off.

Brenna started to give Heath instructions to her loft, so he could drop her off, but she found he already knew how to get there. "You've been there already," she said. "I forgot." The thought of him searching through her things and finding that drawing under her bed, when he didn't even know her, made her uneasy. What had her living space told him about her, other than that she was a thief? Had he examined what brand of mouthwash she used? Had he seen the condoms in her nightstand? Had he read her mail?

He pulled up to the curb, next to an expired meter. It didn't require quarters until morning. "I'll carry your bag up."

"I can get it," she said, trying to match his cool, unemotional tone.

"I want to check your loft before you go in, make sure it's safe. Marvin could have visited while you were gone. He still has his key, doesn't he?"

Brenna nodded, disturbed by the possibility. What if he'd planted more incriminating evidence?

She used a bar code on her key chain to get through the front door—the building had decent security, if nothing else. Then she led Heath down a long, dark hallway to the freight elevator in back.

The first thing she noticed when she opened her door was that her alarm didn't beep. "My security system isn't armed. It's not even turned on."

Heath tensed. "Oh, that. We, um, disabled it."

"You broke my alarm?"

"We'll pay to fix it," he said sheepishly.

She flipped on the light, anxious to see what else had been done to her loft. She stepped inside and turned on all the lights. Then she screamed.

Chapter Ten

Panic rose up in Heath's chest. "What?" He had his gun out, all senses on red alert.

"What happened to my place?" Brenna demanded. "It's totally trashed."

"Um, it was pretty much like this when we arrived."

She turned accusatory eyes on him. "Are you trying to tell me *I* made this hideous mess?"

Brenna strolled through the loft like a general inspecting the troops. She picked up items of clothing and draped them over her arm, grabbed an untidy stack of magazines and tossed them in a trash basket, stacked some dirty dishes sitting on her table. She picked them up, then set them down again and looked at Heath. Now she was the one looking sheepish. "You're right, this is my mess. I'd recognize it anywhere. And I guess there's no hope I could clean it all up before you realized I'm a complete slob."

He couldn't help smiling. "I knew that the first day I met you, when I walked into your room at the Kountry Kozy B&B."

"Hey, no fair. I had lots of help with that mess. But I'm not normally this bad, really. I was just in such a hurry to leave with Sonya and catch Marvin…" She trailed off, sinking onto a crate that served as a chair around a table made out of a giant wooden cable spool. "I'm not sure I can stay here, now that I know the FBI has been all over it. I feel very…"

"Violated?" he offered.

"I was going to say *icky*. But *violated* works. Did they— you—look at *everything?*"

He didn't answer, on the grounds that she wouldn't like it if he did so truthfully. "You'll feel better when it's cleaned up."

"I'm too tired," she said. "I think I'll just get into bed, close my eyes and forget about this nightmare until tomorrow. I'll just see you in the morning sometime."

He was being dismissed. He didn't blame her, really. Maybe tomorrow would be a better day all the way around.

He turned toward the door to let himself out. But just as he was about to make a clean escape, he heard a sound. It sounded sort of like the distressed cry of a baby bird, but more muffled, and he realized with a start that Brenna was crying.

He'd never seen her cry, except after they'd made love, and that was different. He sure as hell couldn't walk away from it.

He returned to the loft's main room to see her still sitting on her crate, leaning over the table, her head cradled in her arms, her shoulders shaking. She hardly made any noise except for that little baby-bird squeak when she inhaled.

Oh, man, he couldn't stand this. He walked over to Brenna, scooped her up off the crate, and carried her to the bed.

"Wh-what are you d-doing?" she managed to ask.

"Putting you to bed. It's been a long, horrible day, and it's time for it to be over."

"It wasn't all…h-horrible," she murmured, clinging to him. She really was about to nod off, like a child who had cried herself to sleep. "I d-don't know why I'm losing it now. I mean, I should be all h-happy. I'm not in j-jail."

He set her on the bed, pulled off her shoes and socks. He remembered how he'd put her nightgown on when she had food poisoning and decided he didn't need to go that far. He yanked the covers back, and she got under them, completely docile. He didn't imagine that was a natural state for Brenna. He'd better enjoy it while he could.

He covered her up, tucking her in.

Her eyes fluttered open. "I'm not normally like this. This is way weird for me."

"I know. Go to sleep."

"Okay. You stay with me."

"I'll stay until you fall asleep."

"Okay."

Unfortunately, she fell asleep instantaneously. Unfortunate because once she was asleep, he had no excuse to stay. But there was something he could do before he left. He could clean the place up, so she wouldn't awaken to chaos.

After taking off his jacket, he started in on the dishes first. She didn't have an automatic dishwasher so he had to do them by hand. Then he went to work putting things back into drawers and cabinets where they belonged. He dusted, swept, vacuumed and mopped. He even unpacked her suitcase and started a load of laundry. She had a washer and dryer tucked away in one corner of the huge loft.

Once he had things tidied up, he could see what a great living/work space Brenna had created. She'd defined her various "rooms" with bright throw rugs and, in the case of her bedroom, a glass-block wall. The scarred wooden floor and raw brick walls added a certain urban charm to the place, as did the beams and pipes in the open ceiling, which Brenna had painted in a palette of bright colors.

Even the kitchen, featuring a mishmash of outdated appliances in clashing hues, had a certain flair.

Her workspace consisted of a couple of long tables along one exposed brick wall. There was some kind of oven-looking device he imagined was used to cast metal, and an antique library card catalogue used for storage.

The whole place radiated Brenna's personality—cheerful, unpretentious, utilitarian with a kind of wacky style. Heath found that he didn't want to leave. He wanted to just sit here and absorb her essence. The thought of driving all the way back to Addison and dealing with a pile of mail and dead houseplants and an overflowing answering machine was distinctly unappealing.

He checked her one more time—sleeping soundly, all scrunched into a ball like a cat on one corner of the queen-size mattress. The rest of the wide expanse of bed looked awfully empty.

No. No way. Brenna might not be an official suspect at this point, but he hadn't exactly solved this case. In fact, his performance had been exceedingly nonproductive. He hadn't even been the one to clear Brenna's name.

He still had no business getting involved with her. For one thing, she was still very confused and vulnerable after the job Marvin did on her. He couldn't take advantage of that.

Friends. That's what she wanted, and he would honor that. It would be best for both of them.

He forced himself to turn out the lights and leave.

WHEN BRENNA AWOKE, it was still early, the sky barely blushing with the coming dawn. But she felt wide-awake and energized. It was time to move forward with her life. Marvin had gotten away, he'd stolen money and stuff from her, but what were money and stuff? She had her health, she had her freedom—a big plus—and she and Heath were going shopping today.

On the way to the bathroom to take a shower, she stopped, realizing something wasn't quite right. Her loft was clean. No trace of last night's horrible mess was visible. In fact, her loft was much cleaner than it had been when she'd left more than a month ago.

Unless the Housekeeper Fairies had arrived last night, Heath had done this. She'd guilted him into it with her semihysteria, but still, how many men would clean your whole place while you slept?

She felt a strange, squiggly sensation around the region of her heart. Was that friendship? Oh, hell, no.

She was falling in love with him.

Quietly she groaned and headed for the shower. She was such a sap.

HEATH WAS NOT SURPRISED to find Supervisory Special Agent Fleming Ketcher in his office at 7:30 a.m. The man lived and breathed his work and expected others to do the same. He didn't appear to have a personal life.

Ketcher looked up from his computer when Heath knocked on his half-open door. "Oh, you. I want a full report of the Brenna Thompson debacle on my desk before noon."

He'd anticipated his boss's request and laid a sheaf of papers on Ketcher's desk. "It's right here." He'd stayed up the rest of the night to produce the report and transcribe the tapes. It had taken him hours to word everything just right. He hadn't included any out-and-out lies, just a few ambiguous bits.

"Dropping the charges against Brenna was the right thing to do," Heath said, at the risk of sounding like he'd once again let an attractive woman wrap him around her little finger. "Marvin Carter framed her."

Ketcher made a disgusted noise. "Marvin Carter. I don't want to hear anything more about some two-bit con man. Do you have any idea how much time, how many man-hours, were wasted on this supposedly stolen Picasso?"

"It was stolen," Heath said. "Just not by Brenna."

Ketcher finally looked up from his computer screen, spearing Heath with a malevolent stare. "Make no mistake, Packer, Brenna Thompson is not innocent. She may have wishy-washy parents and a powerful lawyer, but that doesn't make her innocent. Or are you completely blind to the evidence?"

"It's all in the report," he said, determined not to lose his temper. "So you don't want to even look for the real thief?" Heath supposed he shouldn't be surprised by his supervisor's attitude.

"Why is it so important to you?"

Heath paused, pondering what to say. Finally he settled on, "I need to solve this case. For me."

"And you think finding a stolen Picasso will show the folks back home in Baltimore how well you're doing," Ketcher said snidely.

It wasn't true. Maybe when he'd first opened this investigation, he'd cared about his precious reputation. Now he was more concerned about doing what was right, and that meant putting Marvin behind bars and clearing Brenna's name once and for all. Well, he supposed he didn't want to be fired in disgrace, either, but that was secondary.

"I'll tell you what I want," Ketcher said. "I want to forget this case ever crossed my desk and get back to the War on Terrorism. My job is to keep this country safe, not chase after a womanizing thief."

"In that case, I'd like to take a week of vacation. Starting today."

Ketcher looked up again. By his expression, Heath half expected him to say, *Real men don't take vacations*.

But Ketcher surprised him. "I'll see what I can do. You haven't taken a day off in weeks. Maybe when you come back rested and fresh, you'll do a better job keeping your priorities straight. Marvin Carter," he muttered. "Sheesh."

Heath longed to argue, to make Ketcher understand what a true menace Carter was. But he was afraid his boss would change his mind about the vacation.

"Thanks, Fleming," he said, meaning it. Then he got the hell out of there.

BRENNA KEPT HERSELF BUSY that morning. She consulted her files on the designs she intended to recreate and made more notes and calculations. She made phone calls to see which vendors might be persuaded to extend credit her way. Not many, as it turned out. But she was able to open a new credit card account to replace the one Marvin had trashed.

She also initiated an insurance claim for the stolen jewelry, providing the police reports, detailed descriptions and copies of the designs and estimated values—a task she'd been too disheartened to attend to right after the theft.

While she was keeping her hands and her brain busy, her emotions vibrated just beneath the surface. She was falling in love with Heath. She was headed for another emotional train wreck, no doubt, but the future didn't seem to matter so much. She was too enamored with the present—she was in love.

She tried not to watch the clock, but even so, as it grew closer to noon, she became anxious. What if he didn't show? What if he'd changed his mind? Guys did that.

At 11:15, though, her doorbell rang, and she was so flustered she buzzed her visitor in without even checking who it was. Thank God, it *was* Heath. She opened the door when he was still trudging up the stairs, and drank in the sight of him in faded jeans, a zippered fleece pullover and a bomber jacket.

She liked this look. She liked it so much, in fact, that she struggled to get a grip on herself. No spontaneous displays of affection, she cautioned herself. She might be in love and that was great for her, but she'd learned the hard way that guys were wired a little differently. That emotional bonding thing came a little more slowly for the male of the species. Like forever in her case.

"How'd it go?" she asked, referring to his meeting with his boss. "Any problems?"

"Not unless having a boss who's a jerk is a big problem. The good news is, you're well and truly off the hook. The bad news is, so is Marvin. Catching Marvin has become a low priority."

Brenna just shook her head. She took Heath's jacket and hung it on a hook by the door. "I guess The Blondes are on their own again."

"Not completely. I'm taking a week of vacation, and I'm going to use at least part of that time to track Marvin down."

"You mean you're leaving?" She hated that idea.

"Not unless I get a hot lead. I'll do my tracking by computer and phone. Sometimes finding a fugitive becomes a matter of cyber legwork, the kind of time-consuming, painstaking attention the FBI can't do unless it's a major case."

"You can use my computer," she offered.

"I might take you up on that. So, are you ready to go shopping?"

Brenna cocked her head at him. "That's the first time a guy ever asked me *that*."

Unlike Los Angeles or New York, Dallas didn't have a jewelry district. Shopping for raw materials required zig-zagging all over town. As Heath ferried her here and there, Brenna told him *her* good and bad news.

"I went through my mail and found a couple of consignment checks I hadn't expected. After I paid all my bills, I netted out about even."

"Could be worse," he said.

"I also found a few vendors who would give me thirty days' credit," she said. "And some were willing to work with me on a sort of consignment basis, provided I sign away first- and second-born children."

"Just don't have any children," Heath quipped. "Joke's on them."

Brenna's mischievous imagination conjured up an image of herself with a baby. Heath's baby. And it didn't feel all that strange. She'd always assumed she wouldn't have children because she didn't feel at all maternal. But she supposed that could change under the right circumstances.

Get a grip, Brenna. She'd only just acknowledged that she might be falling in love with Heath, and now she was having his babies? Friends. For now they were just friends. She had to stop rushing willy-nilly into relationships. Heath had already admitted he was helping her out to assuage his guilt. Guilt was not a good basis for a romantic relationship.

She sighed. No time to moon about what could be or might have been. She had work to do.

Their shopping trip was surprisingly fun. Brenna felt like a kid in a candy store, buying large hunks of gold and silver as if it were marshmallow fluff. She also visited an estate jeweler who was willing to sell her some ugly, broken pieces with missing stones at a deep discount. Heath kept pressing his Visa card on her, and eventually she was forced to accept his offer. He seemed pleased to be able to help her.

As she amassed precious and semiprecious stones, she mentally revised some of her designs. By the time they stopped for a late lunch, Brenna was convinced she could do it. She scratched items off her list as she wolfed down a club sandwich.

She was afraid Heath would be bored, but he seemed to be enjoying himself. He just grinned as she chattered inanely about her ideas for a silver-and-turquoise necklace for her sister-in-law, Blair, who was fixated on all things Southwestern. "What's so funny?" she finally asked him.

"You. And I wouldn't say you're funny. You're just a pleasure to watch. So few people in this world have a passion, some vocation or hobby that they can throw themselves into a hundred percent, something that brings them pure bliss. You're the exception."

She allowed herself to fully enjoy the compliment. "Passion I've got. Talent is something else again."

"You're talented," he said. "I thought so when I saw your designs, but when I held that one necklace in New Orleans, I knew it was special."

She sighed. "Seneca—I mean, Marvin—said the same thing to me."

"Just because he lied about some things doesn't mean he lied about everything. The best con men use the truth where they can."

"You think?" she asked, appalled by her need for ego strokes.

"I know. Stop worrying. You're going to be the toast of the IGA show."

"IJC. IGA is a grocery store chain."

"Whatever. Finish your sandwich and let's go. I'm anxious to watch you work."

She laughed, amazed. "You're really serious. It's not very exciting. It's not like they'd ever base a TV show on jewelry makers."

"Viewers would tune in by the millions to watch you."

Brenna's face heated. She was such a sucker for a compliment. Marvin had perceived that about her ten minutes after meeting her, and had used that knowledge to his benefit. She should be suspicious of any man who praised her.

But she wasn't.

Chapter Eleven

Brenna worked at a feverish pace over the next couple of days. Even with the designs and some of the molds already done, thirty pieces of jewelry were still a helluva lot to do in nine days. Her work area got so hot from the constant use of her acetylene torch that she had to strip down to a tank top and gym shorts.

To her absolute shock and delight, Heath was there to assist. She didn't really understand why he'd committed himself to helping her get to the New York show, complete with a suitcase full of jewelry, but she was too busy to question it. He fixed her meals or brought in carryout. He opened her mail and brought to her attention only the really important stuff. He screened her calls, surprising the heck out of her mother.

She sat at her bench each day until her eyes crossed and her hands ached from working the silver and gold. Then she fell into bed, exhausted, and arose the next morning to do it all over again.

Heath went home every night, but reappeared at the crack of dawn, usually with coffee. It was frustrating to have him so near all the time and not touch him, but it was a good exercise in self-control, too. Without sex and all its complications getting in the way, she found herself focusing on other aspects of their relationship—camaraderie, laughter, good conversation about everything in the world.

Heath steadfastly remained a perfect gentleman, which bugged her no end. Maybe she *was* the kind of woman he would only take to bed after a few drinks.

Sometimes Heath sat at her computer, tapping keys in mysterious patterns. He was using various law enforcement databases to search for signs of Marvin, but so far he was having no luck. The man appeared to have gone to ground.

Heath did get a lead on Ardith Smelter, who had used her credit card to withdraw cash at an ATM in Tallahassee, Florida. But all he could do was make a call to the FBI Orlando Field Office and alert the agents there to be on the lookout for her. She had no known ties to that area.

"Maybe you should go there," Brenna suggested, hating the thought. "I can manage by myself."

"If I had a more solid lead to follow, I would," he said. "But Ardith might have just been passing through Tallahassee. The ATM she used was near a major freeway."

Brenna was relieved. Heath's steadying presence was the only thing that kept her from tearing her hair out.

On the third day the phone rang. Brenna, hard at work on a wax model for a ring, ignored it until a minute or so later Heath asked, "Do you want to talk to Cindy Rheems?"

Brenna dropped the heated modeling tool. "Yes! Of course!" She grabbed the phone. "Cindy! How was your honeymoon?"

"Never mind me, who's the hunky social secretary?"

"How do you know he's hunky?"

"He sounds it. So, I haven't even unpacked my suitcase. I'm dying to know. Have you found Marvin?"

"Girlfriend, you wouldn't believe what's been going on since you ran off to Italy." And she filled Cindy in on Sonya's mother's heart attack, finding and losing Ardith at the jewelry show, her own arrest, the missing Picasso. She left out the more personal stuff, though if Heath hadn't been listening while pretending absorption in the computer, she'd have dished.

"So, let me get this straight," Cindy said. "Your parents turned you in as a thief, this FBI agent arrested you, but then the charges were mysteriously dropped."

"Uh-huh."

"And while you're slaving away with your baubles, he's…"

"Bringing me pizza. Doing my laundry."

"And he's doing this because…"

"I don't know."

"Is he getting nooky?" Cindy asked.

"No. Well, once."

Heath's hands slowed on the keyboard, and Brenna knew for sure he was listening, knew he knew what she was talking about.

"But you can't give me the details?" Cindy almost whined.

"Not right now. Cindy, once I get done with the show in New York, I want to keep looking for Marvin."

"Me, too! I'll find out if Sonya's in."

"She will be, once she gets her mother squared away. Of course, she does have a wedding to call off."

"What?"

"I should let her explain it."

"Sounds like you both have a lot of explaining to do."

Brenna could have talked to Cindy all day. Though they'd known each other only a short time, their shared experiences with Marvin had caused all three women to grow as close as sisters. She ached to be with them, to share her fears and her hopes about the upcoming show.

"Could you do one more thing?" she asked before Cindy hung up. "Could you talk to Heath? Tell him about the cash he found in my suitcase."

Heath took the phone, and Brenna listened avidly to the one-sided conversation, which mostly consisted of "Uh-huh…uh-huh." Then he grinned. "I wouldn't *think* of it."

After they hung up, Brenna asked, "You wouldn't think of what?"

"Taking advantage of your vulnerable state."

Darn. She *wanted* to be taken advantage of. "So do you believe me now about where that money came from?"

"I always believed you." At her narrowed eyes, he added, "Okay, not at first. But I wanted to, and you convinced me a long time ago you were telling the truth. Now get back to work."

"Slave driver," Brenna muttered.

"Just protecting my investment."

Her back hurt from hunching over her workbench for so many hours, but she kept at it.

THE MORE HEATH WATCHED Brenna work, the more he realized how wrong her parents had been about her artistic abilities. She wasn't just accomplished; she was inspired. He would watch her take a formless bit of silver and work it this way and that with her torch and her endless variety of shaping tools, trying to guess what it would turn out to be. And he would be completely flummoxed until all at once, a form emerged—a flower, a dragonfly, a crescent moon.

Even more fascinating than watching a beautiful work

of art emerge from chaos was watching Brenna herself. At first she'd been self-conscious with Heath studying her every move, but after a while she'd gotten used to him and, sadly for his ego, forgot about him. She lost herself in the process of creation, focusing so hard on a piece of precious metal that he thought she must be forming it with her mind power as much as with her tools. Then she would look up, dazed, shocked to realize four or five hours had passed during which she'd been oblivious to the world.

Sometimes he worked at the computer, trying every trick he knew to track down Marvin. He continued chasing down every Marvin Carter he could find, to no avail. He tried again with the one in Boston, the millionaire's son, wanting to at least let him know a con man was using his identity. But he wasn't able to locate *that* Marvin, whose blue-blooded parents reported that he was vacationing in the Far East.

Marvin hadn't been back in contact with Shelly Bernard, the Louisiana bank teller who'd briefly been his lover. He hadn't recently used any of the credit cards he'd stolen—he'd gotten too smart for that.

Brenna gave Heath a key to her loft and the security code, so he could come and go. He lectured her that she shouldn't be so trusting, while at the same time he enjoyed having her trust. He remembered all too well those accusing blue eyes of hers in his rearview mirror on the drive back to Dallas, and he didn't care to ever again see them directed at him.

On the fifth day of Brenna's jewelry-making marathon, Heath was going through his daily Marvin-hunting routine on the computer. By now he was so used to finding nothing that he was startled to see that Marvin's cell phone had been used. The account had been deactivated weeks ago for nonpayment, but now the number was working again.

He didn't tell Brenna right away. He wanted to see how much information he could dig up. Besides, she was so involved in hammering a piece of silver on her tiny anvil that he didn't want to interrupt her. After some digging, he determined that the calls—four of them—had originated from different towns along the Florida Interstate. So Marvin was still on the move and possibly with Ardith.

As for who had received the calls—several used-car dealers. Marvin was shopping, apparently. But when Heath contacted all the dealers, they weren't very helpful.

Heath had an idea, though. He waited until Brenna stopped long enough to drink some bottled water.

"Brenna?"

She jumped. "Yes?"

"Did you ever do any acting?"

"Me? No. I could never memorize lines. In the school play I got to play a dead body. But I couldn't even do that right. I got the hiccups. Why?"

He told her about what he'd learned, and she got very excited. "He's getting careless! Maybe we should go to Florida."

"You have jewelry to make."

She deflated a little at that. "If we found Marvin and recovered my jewelry—"

"There's no guarantee he still has your jewelry," Heath said gently, taking her by the hand and leading her to the sofa, a brown, nubby thing, soft and comfortably worn. "He was already trying to sell it in New Orleans. Anyway, I have an idea. But it's going to require you to play a part."

She was already shaking her head. "It'll never work. I'm terrible at acting."

"We'll write you out a script, so you won't have to memorize anything. We'll rehearse it."

She got a very wary look in her eye. "You want me to call him, don't you?"

Heath nodded. "If you could set up a meeting—"

"That won't work! The minute he hears my voice he'll hang up and never use that cell number again."

"I'm not so sure. Hear me out. We know some things about Marvin. One is that he thinks he's very smart, much smarter than the women he's fleecing. He's got a king-size ego and enough nerve to fill Texas Stadium."

"And he's greedy, let's not forget that."

"Right. We can use what we know against him."

"How?"

"We make him believe you were so enamored with him, you can't conceive that he stole from you. You think someone else must be responsible. You think *you* did something to drive him away, and you'll do *anything* to win back his love."

"Oh, yuck."

"He'll lap it up with a spoon."

"But he doesn't want me back," Brenna objected. "And I have nothing left to steal."

"So we lure him to you with a prize so tempting he can't stand to turn it down. What's the only thing he really wants?"

"Cold, hard cash, apparently. I mean, I can't see him hanging that Picasso on his wall and admiring it. He sold his car, my jewelry, Cindy's restaurant…"

Heath thought for a minute. "How easy is it to sell a stolen Picasso, I wonder?" He could tell by the light in Brenna's eyes that she saw the possibilities.

They did some brainstorming, script-writing and rehearsing. Finally Brenna agreed she was as ready as she'd ever be. She dialed Marvin's reactivated cell number and waited for him to answer.

Heath leaned in close so he could hear both sides of the conversation. He was holding the script, ready to prompt Brenna if she got stuck.

"Todd Baker," a male voice answered. "Hello?"

The strange name threw Brenna for a moment, but she recovered quickly. "I'm looking for Mr. Seneca Dealy."

"Brenna?"

"Yes! It's me! Don't hang up, okay? I just want to talk to you. Oh, Sen, I miss you."

Heath cringed. Brenna wasn't kidding—she really was a bad actress, especially if he watched her face. But with his eyes closed it was better—still a bad soap opera, but not *Saturday Night Live*.

"You do, huh?" Marvin sounded curious. Good. He gave an encouraging nod to Brenna.

"I don't know what I did to drive you away, but whatever it is, I'm sorry. I tried to give you some time—maybe we were together too much. Maybe I smothered you."

"I was feeling a bit overwhelmed," he said. "What went on between us was so powerful."

Brenna made a gagging gesture. "Yes! Yes, it was. Oh, Seneca, something awful has happened. I've been the victim of a theft! It happened the day y—our last day together," she quickly amended. Heath nodded again. He'd cautioned Brenna not to say anything that could be construed as laying blame on Marvin. "They stole all my money and my jewelry, too. I had to pull out of the IJC show."

"Oh, Brenna, how terrible! Do the police have any leads?"

"Well, some awful woman named Alice was trying to sell my necklace in New Orleans. But she got away."

"Honey, if I'd known—God, it must have been terrible, going through such a loss all alone. Was your family any help at all?"

"Of course not. They all hate me. And I hate them. That's why I was glad—well, I'm glad they suffered a loss, too. It was no more than they deserved." She paused, waiting.

"So, what happened?"

Marvin wouldn't admit to any wrongdoing, especially not on the phone. Heath had expected as much.

"You know what happened!" she said playfully. "I made it easy for you. And I'm very grateful you took the hint. But shouldn't I get, like, a percentage? A finder's fee?"

"I'm not sure what you're talking about," Marvin said with exaggerated innocence.

Brenna made a face at the phone. "Ohhhh, I get it. Right. Mum's the word. But I happen to know an art collector with a very large bankroll who is not too fussy about where his paintings come from, if you get my drift."

"Brenna," Marvin said sharply, "let's not talk about business. God, I've missed you. I want to see you."

"Oh, I'd like that." Brenna was bouncing up and down on the sofa, she was so excited. "Where are you?"

"Far away, unfortunately, or I'd come over there right now. Can you wait till next week? Maybe Friday?"

Perfect, Heath thought. They could deal with it after Brenna's trip to New York.

"Friday would work." They nailed down a meeting time and place.

"I still love you, darling." With that Marvin hung up.

"Oh, my God!" Brenna screamed. "We did it! He went for it! You can call in a SWAT team and nab him the minute he shows."

Heath was grinning, too. "You were splendid. A terrible liar, but you didn't lose your nerve."

"Was I that awful?"

"We're just lucky he couldn't see your face."

ELATION TURNED TO DESPAIR the next morning. It was Day Six, and Brenna had only nine pieces of jewelry completely finished. She had rough settings for about a dozen more, awaiting the painstaking grinding and polishing that would create the mirror sheen she demanded.

"I'm not going to make it," she declared glumly as she desultorily ate a bowl of Cheerios.

"Don't say that. Of course you'll make it." Heath wasn't as confident as he tried to sound. He hadn't dreamed how time-consuming and difficult making works of art like Brenna's could be.

"Do the math. I've got three days left till I have to board the plane for New York. I could maybe rough out the nine pieces I need, but the finishing work—I'll never get it all done."

"What if you had help?"

"We've already determined that's not an option," she said, not unkindly. It was true, he'd tried to help her once, but his great big hands were a menace to her delicate pieces of jewelry. He'd tried to solder a clasp onto the back of a brooch and had wound up with a big glob of metal that went all over everything, and had burned himself to boot.

"Not me," he said. "But isn't there someone else you could call? What about one of your sisters?"

Brenna laughed. "They're all still mad at me for 'stealing' Grandma's jewelry. Even if they were inclined to help, they all work, or have kids, or both. And not an artistic bone among them."

"What about friends? Hey, how about The Blondes?"

Brenna's eyes widened, then her face lit up. "I forgot all about Cindy and Sonya. Oh, but I don't know if I could ask them—"

"Of course you could. They're your friends. They'll help if they can. Cindy loves to travel and experience new things, you told me. She would jump at the chance to be part of this."

"But Sonya has a sick mother."

"Just ask her. Maybe she needs to get away for a weekend."

"Okay. Okay, I'll ask them." She set down her spoon, got up, and strode to the phone in the kitchen.

"Uh, Brenna? It's not even six in the morning."

"Oh. I guess I'll wait a couple of hours."

BRENNA WORKED like the furies of hell were after her, but Heath knew it was because she once again had hope. The blond cavalry was on its way. Heath had been right; Cindy and Sonya had jumped at the chance to help her any way they could. Cindy was bringing her fifteen-month-old son, Adam, and Sonya was bringing her bodyguard, the mysterious John-Michael McPhee. It would be an interesting couple of days.

They arrived together later that afternoon, and the three women shrieked with delight at being reunited and once again having a common purpose.

"How is your mother?" Heath politely asked Sonya.

Sonya smiled. "She's doing much better. I convinced her I needed to travel to Dallas to personally select the Belgian lace for my train."

Heath's head was spinning. "Wait a minute. Your mother *still* thinks you're getting married?" he asked.

"Yes," Sonya answered without apology. "And she's going to continue thinking it awhile longer. When her doctor says she's well enough to withstand a terrible shock— and it will be terrible, trust me—I'll tell her the truth."

Heath just shook his head. He wasn't sure he approved

of duping Sonya's poor mother. But he wasn't exactly the prince of honesty himself.

"Wait a minute," Brenna said as she reacquainted herself with Cindy's little boy, giving him enthusiastic hugs and messy kisses that made him giggle uncontrollably. "Aren't we missing someone? Where's John-Michael, the sexy bodyguard?"

Sonya's mouth firmed and she refused to talk about it, so Cindy stepped in. "You should have been on the ride up here. John-Michael was driving the limo, and Sonya never said a word to him the whole way."

Obviously something was up with Sonya and her bodyguard, Heath mused. Brenna would no doubt pry it out of her later. "I'll go talk to him," he said, a little curious himself. He wanted to reacquaint himself with the man who'd shown such cool in New Orleans, when they'd both been caught someplace they shouldn't have been.

TWO SECONDS AFTER the door closed behind Heath, Brenna's friends were on her. "So what gives?" Cindy demanded. "Why do you have an FBI agent living with you?"

"He looks even better in those faded jeans than he did in a suit," Sonya said with a delicate shiver. "You can't tell me he's 'just a friend.'"

"He's just a friend," Brenna confirmed. "He keeps the loft clean and the fridge stocked while I work, but he sleeps at his own place every night."

"Marry him," Cindy said. "Guys who don't leave a mess in their wake are hard to find."

"Marry him, right," Brenna said. "He's not interested."

"Then why is he here?" Cindy asked, perplexed.

"I don't know. Guilt is my best guess. He seduced me, then arrested me."

"*He* seduced *you?*" Cindy asked skeptically.

Both women crossed their arms and stared at Brenna. Even Adam, who couldn't possibly understand what they were talking about, stared at her as if expecting an answer, now.

Brenna caved and told them about their uninhibited lovemaking in a New Orleans garden.

"So was it good?" Sonya asked, clearly delighted by the prurient details of the story. "Or do you remember?"

"*I* remember all of it," Brenna said dreamily. "Those Hurricanes might have erased his inhibitions, but they didn't affect his performance."

"Woo-hoo!" Cindy called out, doing a little bump and grind, which made Adam stare in wide-eyed wonder. "Sounds like you caught a live one."

"I didn't catch him," Brenna said. "He slipped off the righteous path for one night. He said in specific terms that he made a terrible mistake and it wouldn't happen again."

"But he's here, isn't he?" Sonya pointed out. "Guilt only carries a man so far."

"If he's sweeping and dusting, he's got a baaaaad case for you," Cindy concurred. "Maybe we can figure out what's up with him if we observe him the next couple of days. Meanwhile, don't we have some work to do?"

"Work, right." Brenna had been so delighted to see her friends again, so relieved to be able to confide in someone, that she'd all but forgotten the main reason they were here.

She'd organized everything before her friends had arrived. Neither of them claimed to be artistic, but Sonya was the one with—surprisingly—the engineering degree. So although jewelry making had little to do with petroleum exploration and extraction, Brenna put Sonya to work with her set of tiny files. She had files of every conceivable shape and size as well as a motorized grinder for working larger areas. Sonya was a quick study and had clever, dexterous hands, even with the acrylic fingernails.

Brenna put Cindy to work polishing. She claimed all the dough kneading she'd done over the years working at the Miracle Café in Cottonwood had prepared her for mindless tasks requiring strong hands, and she took to the job with the precision of water dripping on a rough rock—slow, patient, until she achieved the satin-smooth finish required.

Adam was perfectly happy in his playpen with his blocks, or watching a video, or wandering around the loft once Cindy got it childproofed. Every couple of hours Cindy paused to play with him a few minutes, or feed him or change his diaper. But by and large he was a low-maintenance kid.

While they worked, Brenna filled her compatriots in on the plan she and Heath had hatched to catch Marvin.

"Do you think he'll show?" Cindy asked excitedly.

"For the chance to unload the Picasso, no questions asked? Yeah, I think he'll show." The possibility of finally attaining justice where Marvin was concerned energized them all. Brenna was astounded by the progress they made as a team.

Heath made himself scarce.

"I guess the three of us together are a frightening force," Cindy joked.

"I doubt he's afraid of us," Sonya scoffed. "It's just that he's found a kindred spirit in John-Michael. I'll bet the two of them are off tipping a few brews and telling stories about us."

Brenna focused on her latest design, which would eventually be the humongo engagement ring her sister Helen had always longed for. As Brenna worked on a delicately scrolled platinum band, she pondered Heath's absence. Was he really hanging out with John-Michael? Was he dishing, the way she'd done with her girlfriends? She supposed she couldn't condemn him if he was, since she hadn't spared many details with Sonya and Cindy. The story about stripping down in a garden and making love on a stone bench was just too funny—and oddly, romantic—to keep to herself.

But she didn't imagine Heath would blab. He seemed too private. He still hadn't told her what had happened in Baltimore that caused him to transfer to Dallas, the thing that had tarnished his reputation, the thing she still suspected had something to do with a woman.

Chapter Twelve

That night Brenna's apartment reminded her of her college days, with sleeping bodies strewn everywhere and half-eaten bags of tortilla chips lying about. Sonya and Brenna shared the bed; Cindy had brought her sleeping bag and an air mattress and was snoozing peacefully in a corner of the dining room. Adam was curled up in his playpen nearby. Because they'd all worked so late, Sonya and Cindy had convinced Heath to sleep on the couch.

After lots of pressure from her friends, Sonya had relented and invited John-Michael to join the party, but he'd declined, his feathers ruffled from her earlier treatment, and he'd gone to a hotel. Probably a smart move. He would have had to sleep in a chair or on the hard floor if he'd stayed here.

Heath made a deli run the next morning, and everyone gorged on bagels and sweet rolls. They worked hard through the morning. Brenna focused on setting stones into the polished settings. She showed Sonya how to cut chains and attach clasps for the necklaces, and Cindy tried her hand at soldering, with a bit more success than Heath. Heath, for his part, kept them fed and kept Adam totally enthralled.

Every so often, Brenna looked up from her workbench to watch Heath and Adam. Heath appeared to be a natural with kids. He made funny faces and swung Adam around with no embarrassment. Adam took to Heath with all the enthusiasm of a puppy with a new toy.

"They do look cute together," Cindy whispered covertly to Brenna, causing Brenna to jump. She hadn't realized she'd been observed. "Doesn't it just make you want to run out and have one of your own?"

"Bite your tongue," Brenna said. Heath had used a condom in New Orleans, but what if it hadn't done its job? Condoms did sometimes fail. Heath would probably be a great dad. But thrusting him into the role of reluctant father wasn't the way to do it.

BY LATE THAT EVENING it was done. All of it. Brenna put all thirty pieces inside her display cases, thankful she'd invested in nice ones last year. The jewelry rested in a sculpted sea of blue-gray velvet. She filled in any empty-looking spots with some of her best silver charms, which Marvin hadn't bothered to steal. To get the full effect, she hung up her sign, which was a work of art unto itself, made with layers of black, silver and electric blue Plexiglas outlined in neon. It said simply, Brenna.

Her friends stood around the display wearing appropriate expressions of awe and admiration, which Brenna soaked up. She needed the validation.

"I want that one," Sonya declared, pointing to the engagement ring, which currently sported an amethyst instead of a diamond. "Except I can't afford it," she added glumly.

"It's not for sale, anyway," Brenna said. "It's going to my sister."

"Well," Sonya said, "after your trip to New York, if you have any pieces left, you could show them to my mom. She would love these."

Brenna's heart beat a little faster at the thought of Muffy Patterson wearing Brenna's jewelry to her society functions and telling everyone where she got it. Muffy was very influential in Houston's upper crust.

She would worry about that later. Right now, her friends were leaving, and she didn't know how to begin to thank them.

"I don't know what to say." She held out her hands to Cindy and Sonya in supplication. "You guys are the best friends anyone could wish for."

Cindy and Sonya hugged her in turn. "You'd do the same for either of us," Cindy said. "Remember how you took Adam and me in when I was homeless, no questions?"

"You can thank us by being the star of the show," Sonya added.

"I hardly think I'll be the star," Brenna said. "All the famous designers will be there, the ones that get full-page ads in *Vogue*."

"They had to start somewhere," Cindy said encouragingly.

After her friends left, Heath went out on some mysterious errand, and Brenna was alone in the loft for the first time in a long time. It seemed preternaturally quiet without Adam's chatter and the buzz and whir of grinders and the acetylene torch.

She stepped back and looked critically at her work. Could it possibly measure up? Or would they laugh at her? She knew she was too close to her own work to properly judge it. One minute she thought her pieces were brilliant, and the next all she could see were the flaws. The thought of putting herself out there, opening herself to criticism, scared her silly. Yet if she didn't risk it now, would she ever?

"It looks like sunlight glinting off the ocean after a storm."

Brenna jumped when she realized Heath had re-entered the apartment without alerting her. "That's an unusually poetic observation from you. Where've you been?"

He set a brown bag on her spool table and ripped it open dramatically, revealing a bottle of merlot. "I think we need to celebrate." He stood several feet from her, hesitating to come any closer.

Brenna didn't hesitate. She walked over, took his hand between both of hers. "I couldn't have finished without you."

"I didn't do anything."

"Oh, yeah, right. Mr. Modest." She threw her arms around his neck, stood on her toes and kissed him. He tried at first to resist her, standing like a totem pole, completely unresponsive. But there was one reaction he couldn't disguise. Brenna felt his arousal pressing against her belly through several layers of clothes. Taking full advantage, she rubbed herself against his desire.

The rest of him came to life. He entwined his fingers in her short hair, grabbing a handful and using it to tip her head back so he could return her kiss the way he wanted to.

"Brenna," he groaned against her mouth. "I'm not sure we're ready for this."

"I know, but I can't help it."

"I'm not—" He stopped.

"You're not what? That kind of boy?" she teased. But

then she got serious. "This is our last night together. Tomorrow I'm going to New York. After that, who knows? You'll be back to work, surveilling someone else, and we'll have lost the opportunity."

"If and when we want to make love, we can make the opportunity," he said with far too much reason. "We don't have to wait for one to just happen."

And that, she realized, was the problem. She was afraid once he'd distanced himself physically from her, he wouldn't make the opportunity. It was a pattern she'd fallen into time and again—believing she wasn't worth the effort.

"Are you hungry?" he asked, easing away from her. "I could probably rustle up a frozen pizza."

"Trying to distract me with food is dirty pool."

"Whatever works." He turned toward the kitchen.

"Heath?"

He stopped, his back rigid. "What?"

"I love you. If that makes any difference." She couldn't believe she'd just said that. Her whole life she'd been falling for guys and blurting out her raw, untempered feelings, at which point they immediately lost interest. Or they told her they loved her, but only long enough to get into her pants.

She hadn't learned her lesson yet, apparently. But she'd never been one to hold back when she was feeling something.

He turned slowly, and she dreaded what she might see in his eyes. Disgust? Or worse, pity?

Her heart did a big swoop. What she saw in his eyes was a fire that answered her own, a need so naked and primal it almost screamed. In two steps he returned to her and he was kissing her in a way that was different from before.

He wasn't holding back, and the full force of his desire ran over her like a steamroller. She was melting like her silver under the acetylene torch, completely malleable. He could have bent her, folded her, flattened her, made her anything he wanted.

What he chose to do was lift her up and carry her to the bed.

This wasn't how things usually worked, she thought dazedly as she and Heath tugged on each other's clothes. Usually, if you told a guy you loved him, he got this shifty look on his face, cleared his throat a few times and headed for the hills. She'd only said it because she'd figured she didn't have anything to lose. And because she really meant it, of course.

She did love him. She'd thought and thought about why he was doing so much to help her, and she'd finally realized there could be no other reason except that he wanted to. How could she not love a guy as selfless as that?

In a few short minutes he had her stripped down to nothing but her panties. Her efforts hadn't been quite as effectual; Heath was still wearing his jeans. But he remedied that situation, and soon he was lying beside her.

She trembled with anticipation. He thought she was cold and drew the blankets up over both of them. "Better?" he whispered.

"It couldn't get better."

"We'll make this work somehow," he murmured in her ear. He covered her face and throat with kisses while running his hands up and down her body as if she were a sleek cat.

Later, she would worry about how to make it work in the long run. Right now, she wanted to revel in the moment. She finally had Heath in her bed again, only this time they were both sober.

He'd been an enthusiastic and generous lover under the influence of Hurricanes. Sober, he was still enthusiastic and generous, but with a lot more finesse. He teased and explored, trying a touch here, a kiss there, a tickle of breath somewhere else, taking careful note of what made her gasp with pleasure and repeating often.

Brenna had often been told she was "good in bed," which she hadn't taken too seriously. She figured it meant only that it was good she was in bed at all. Now she knew what that phrase meant, and her efforts to keep apace were paltry at best. Though Heath was obviously aware when she touched him in certain ways, moaning with pleasure, he never became distracted from his own agenda, which apparently was to reduce Brenna to a quivering heap of Jell-O.

The panties came off. Heath coaxed her legs apart and caressed her, his fingers sliding in and out of her as her juices flowed. It was obvious to both of them she was more than ready.

Belatedly she remembered birth control. Her ability to speak was severely compromised, but with grunts and gestures she managed to get across to Heath that he should open the drawer of her nightstand. He groped around and finally found a string of foil packets. She took the string of packets from him, separated one from the herd, ripped it open with her teeth.

He ran a teasing finger over her bottom while she tried to gracefully sheath him. She giggled. "Let me do this. It's a delicate operation. You wouldn't want it to end up over your big toe, would you?"

He relented, cooperating meekly enough. But the second he was sheathed, he flipped her onto her back with no effort, a predatory look in his eye. The teasing was over, she realized as a wave of anticipation washed over her.

He entered her with maddening slowness. This was nothing like the crazy, rushed lovemaking in the garden. Though they were both near the breaking point, Heath still managed to draw their lovemaking out to an almost painfully leisurely pace. When she tried to go faster, thrusting her pelvis up to envelop him deeply inside her, he placed one hand on either hip bone and held her firmly against the mattress.

He was going to set the pace, and she was a helpless, whimpering victim.

He built the pressure within her until she knew she would explode. Inevitably, though, he reached a point where his own need overcame his self-control. His eyes closed, his face contorted, he plunged into her with heated abandon. The exquisite pressure and friction and heat made her toss her head from side to side with a complete lack of control, which finally culminated in a crashing peak of pleasure.

Her cries of ecstasy seemed to spur him on, and with a few final, deep thrusts, his cries mingled with hers.

Afterward the silence in the loft was deafening. Brenna clung to Heath, never wanting to let him go. She'd never felt so blissful, and yet she wanted to cry.

He was so tender as he held her, neither of them speaking, but his gentle caresses and light kisses were more effective than any words could have been. She'd never felt so cherished.

A few minutes later Brenna's stomach growled.

"I knew that was coming," Heath teased her.

"Food tastes better right after sex. Want to raid the refrigerator?"

"I'm right behind you."

They pulled on just enough clothes that they wouldn't

freeze, then poked through the fridge and various cabinets until they came up with a smorgasbord of cheese and crackers, a pear, a can of seasoned almonds, and Twinkies, all washed down with flat ginger ale.

Brenna had never enjoyed a meal more.

She watched for signs that Heath was withdrawing, as he had after the first time they'd made love, but she didn't see any yet. Of course, it was still nighttime. In the cold light of day it might be a different story. But for now, he was smiling and relaxed. He even pulled her into his lap as they ate, nuzzling her ear, popping almonds into her mouth.

She decided to take advantage of his rare mood. She was taking a risk in spoiling the congenial atmosphere, she knew, but she might not get another chance.

And she needed to know.

"Heath, can you tell me now, what happened with you back in Baltimore?"

He tensed, but only slightly. "I probably should have told you earlier," he said. "Maybe it would have helped you understand what was going on with me." He took a deep breath. "Okay, here goes. I was married once."

Ah. So it *was* a woman. "Was it not happy?" she asked.

"I thought it was a good marriage. That is, until my colleagues showed up at my door. My ex-wife is in a federal prison for credit card fraud, forgery and multiple counts of theft."

Good gravy. "Did you put her there?" she asked, feeling uneasy. If he could arrest his own wife, why did he ever hesitate to throw the book at Brenna?

"No. Quite the opposite. I enabled her to get away with her crimes for far longer than would have been possible otherwise."

"I don't believe it. Are you saying you were an accomplice?"

"No. I was a completely ignorant dope who was blind to the evidence sitting right in front of my face. The signs were there. I knew she was a shopping addict. If I'd bothered to add up the cost of the things she brought home from the stores, the things that constantly arrived by UPS, I would have realized there was no way she was paying for them on my salary. But she convinced me she got everything on sale, closeout, half-price, whatever.

"And I kept paying this one credit card every month, barely keeping up with the minimum payments, not knowing she had a wallet full of them in different names, checkbooks that didn't belong to her, fake IDs, lines of credit everywhere, including an equity loan against our house that I knew nothing about."

Brenna was horrified. How could a wife do that to her husband?

"Even then, sometimes she just out-and-out shoplifted," he continued. "When she wanted something, there were no barriers high enough to keep her from it. She rented a storage locker where she stored a lot of the stuff, so I would never see it."

"Was she intending to sell it or what?" Brenna asked, confused. "I mean, what was the point of buying stuff she had to hide away?"

"Her defense attorney said it was an illness, and I believe it. But even if she was ill, she knew what she was doing was wrong."

"How did she finally get caught?"

"With a lizard-skin belt under her coat and no receipt. The house of cards fell in on her."

"It must have been awful," Brenna said, meaning it.

"It was bad. But it got worse. Suspicion fell on me. There was a big investigation. No one could believe Christine had racked up hundreds of thousands of dollars in fraudulent debt without my help, or at least my knowledge. But in the end, they couldn't prove I knew. They couldn't find a single signature or fingerprint on a check or a receipt to connect me to it. So they never filed charges against me."

"But the suspicion didn't go away."

"No. That was why I requested a transfer. Only I didn't request to work here under Ketcher. That was someone else's idea. If I knew who, I would…I don't know. Let the air out of their tires."

Brenna laughed at that. She had expected a much more dire threat. But she suspected Heath wasn't the vengeful sort, and even if he'd known who had it in for him at the Bureau, he probably wouldn't do anything worse than a practical joke. She liked that about him. She liked that he hadn't gone all Rambo on her.

After their feast, they returned to Brenna's rumpled bed and made love again in a languid, peaceful way that left Brenna feeling warm and cherished. They fell asleep wrapped around each other.

HEATH WAS IN a deep, dreamless sleep when a loud knocking jerked him to uncomfortable awareness. It took him a moment to remember where he was. When he did, a sense of peace stole over him. Maybe it wasn't his most brilliant decision to jump into bed again with Brenna Thompson, but he didn't regret it. No matter what happened, he wouldn't ever regret it.

The knocking came again and Brenna stirred. "What in the…?"

"You expecting company?"

"No. Anyway, no one can get to my front door without going through the security door first. It must be one of my neighbors." She looked around for something to cover herself with, finally settling on a pair of sweatpants and a T-shirt. Heath scrambled into his jeans. One thing about a loft—you couldn't hide very easily. He hoped it wasn't Brenna's parents at the door.

"Hold your horses, I'm coming!" she yelled as she fished under the bed for a pair of pink fluffy slippers and scuffed her way to the door. He recalled seeing those slippers when he'd searched her loft and thinking how incongruous it was—an art thief who wore pink fuzzy slippers and slept in a Tweety Bird nightshirt.

Heath stayed in the bedroom area, marginally hidden from view by the glass-block wall. No sense advertising his presence to whomever had come calling. But he peeked around the corner and listened intently as Brenna opened the door.

At first he heard only a quiet, male voice, the words indistinguishable. But Brenna's response was loud and unmistakable. "No, you can't come in! What is this?"

Heath leaped into action, retrieving his gun from Brenna's safe, where he'd locked it away while she had a child in the loft. By the time he had the automatic in his hand, however, he recognized the voices of the intruders, who had entered the loft over Brenna's vociferous objections. Ed Rankle, Patty Speers, Pete LaJolla. His fellow agents, his brethren—along with SSA Ketcher himself. Heath laid the gun down, but his heartbeat still accelerated to twice its normal rate.

What was going on, that Fleming Ketcher would rouse himself out of bed at this ungodly hour?

He turned to face the unsmiling agents. Patty already had a subdued Brenna in cuffs, and now they were all looking at him.

Fleming Ketcher, whose generic, bespectacled, slightly doughy looks had once been an asset when he'd worked undercover, turned to Patty, who at least had the good grace to appear uneasy with the situation. "Speers, take Ms. Thompson downstairs and put her in your car."

"What have I done?" Brenna asked, bewildered. "I thought the charges were dropped."

"Let me refresh your memory, Ms. Thompson." Ketcher pulled a piece of paper from his pocket and read aloud in a falsetto voice. "'If I happened to know someone with a certain object he might like to sell, I might be inclined to introduce that someone to an art collector I know with a very large bankroll who is not too fussy about where his paintings come from, if you get my drift.' Sound familiar?"

"My phone was tapped?" Brenna looked straight at Heath, and as always, her feelings showed crystal clear on her face. She thought this was his doing. She thought he had betrayed her.

He opened his mouth to protest, to let her know this was as big a surprise to him as it was to her. But before he could say anything, Patty Speers hustled Brenna out the door.

Heath turned to his boss. "Can I ask just what the hell is going on here?"

"Shouldn't that be my question?" Ketcher asked with an unfriendly smile. "You've been acting a little strange ever since you first came into contact with Ms. Brenna Thompson. When you continually refused to bring her in for questioning, I became suspicious. So I had you watched."

Heath mentally groaned. He should have known Ketcher had something up his sleeve when the charges against Brenna were so cavalierly dropped.

"It appears my suspicions were well-founded," Ketcher continued, a distinctively triumphant note in his voice. "You're sleeping with a suspect."

"I didn't know she was still a suspect," Heath said through his clenched teeth, "since you chose to mislead me about her status."

"Oh. I see. And you didn't know anything about Brenna trying to help her lover—her *other* lover, I should say—fence a stolen Picasso? We know you were in this apartment at the time she made the phone call, so don't bother lying. Did you line up the buyer? In return for the promise of a cut?"

"Of course I was here when she made the call!" Heath exploded. "I set the whole thing up. Since you told me you pulled the plug on the case, I was working it on my own time. I located Marvin through his cell phone records. We were setting up a sting. Did you listen to the tape?"

"I read the transcript."

"Listen to the tape," Heath said. "Brenna is the worst actress in the world. And look—if you'll look over on that table, you'll find the script we worked out so Marvin would trust her."

Ed Larkin picked up the loose-leaf pages of Brenna's telephone script, scanning them with casual interest.

"Brenna didn't do anything wrong," Heath insisted.

The smirk never left Ketcher's face. "Oh, really?" He idly walked over to Brenna's display cases, which still held the newly created jewelry. "Insurance fraud is a crime, last time I checked. Rankle, didn't you say Ms. Thompson had filed an insurance claim on some jewelry? Jewelry that looked a lot like this stuff here?"

"That's not the jewelry that was stolen," Heath objected. "This is new work."

But his arguments were ignored. Ketcher glanced over
at LaJolla and Rankle in some type of prearranged signal.
The two agents came forward.

"Sorry, Packer, but you're under arrest, too."

Chapter Thirteen

Brenna was in a state of shock as the female agent escorted her down four flights of stairs, where a big, black car awaited her. It was a nicer version of Heath's FBI-mobile.

Unfortunately, she had to run the gamut of reporters with microphones in order to reach the dubious safety of the sedan.

"Did you take the Picasso, Ms. Thompson?"

Brenna didn't dignify the stupid question with a denial. Did they really think she was going to say yes, even if she'd done it? It really galled her to see the press here. Obviously they'd been summoned.

The female agent put Brenna in the backseat, closing the door firmly. Cameras continued to jockey for position, shooting stills and video through the window. Knowing she shouldn't, Brenna stuck her tongue out at the photographers, then slumped down in the seat and turned her head.

The agent climbed into the passenger seat, and shut out the keen November wind.

"It's going to be a cold one today," she said in a friendly tone, as if they were heading off for breakfast.

"You must be the good cop."

"Pardon?"

"You know, good cop/bad cop. They sent you downstairs with me because you're a woman, and they think I'll confide my sins to another woman."

The agent neither confirmed nor denied.

"And, for the record, if there are any recording devices in this car, I haven't had my rights read to me. Not that I'm going to say anything incriminating, because I have nothing to confess."

The agent was silent for a while. Finally she offered, "My name's Patty."

"I'm not going to be your friend, Patty, so give it up."

"I know. I just thought you might want to know my name." She paused, then continued. "I like Heath. I've liked him since he first started here in Dallas. I hate what's happened."

"You and me both. Were the reporters his idea?"

Patty didn't answer. Brenna suspected she was under orders to elicit information, not provide it. But her silence said a lot.

"I can't believe he eavesdropped on my private phone conversations." She mentally reviewed what she'd talked about on her phone. Thank God she hadn't gone into intimate details about her and Heath when she'd talked to Cindy and Sonya.

Brenna thought about the past seven days of grueling work that had all been for nothing. She wasn't going to New York. Her flight was at seven that evening. She didn't imagine the FBI was going to let her go, even if she got her mother to write her a note. They didn't organize 6 a.m. raids without some pretty heavy plans.

Oddly, though, the fact that her career dreams were up in smoke didn't bother her nearly as much as Heath's betrayal. How long had he been planning the arrest? Had sleeping with her been part of the plan, or had that come as a happy bonus? The FBI must not care about that kind of propriety, she mused grimly. They would probably look the other way.

And to think she'd been feeling sorry for him last night when he'd told her the story of his ex-wife. It was probably all made up, she decided. Maybe he'd had a plan to create some sort of phony bond with her so she would confide in him.

The older man who'd done all the talking upstairs— Brenna didn't remember his name, he'd flashed his badge so fast—emerged from her building's front door a few minutes later, looking pleased as punch. He spoke genially to the media, who were still parked on the sidewalk, drawing a small crowd as commuters began arriving downtown for work.

Agent Patty's cell phone rang. After a murmured conversation, she maneuvered herself into the driver's seat.

"Where are we going?" Brenna asked.

"To the FBI office. They'll question you there."

"Will Agent Packer question me?" Brenna thought about the fun she could have. No matter what he asked her, she could bring her answer back around to the fact that they'd had sex—three times. They would never want to use the tape of that interview in open court. But the possibility brought her no amusement. She'd promised Heath she wouldn't talk about their liaison. And just because he'd sunk to a new level of sneakiness didn't mean she wasn't bound by her own promises.

Besides, she didn't want the whole world to know what a loose woman she was.

Brenna was fingerprinted and photographed, with

Agent Patty doing the honors this time. It wasn't nearly as much fun. No wonder mug shots always looked so horrible, if they dragged people out of bed and stuck them in front of the camera before they had a chance to drink some coffee.

After she was processed, she was allowed to contact her parents, who promised to arrange for a lawyer. "Not James Prince this time," she cautioned them. James had apparently overlooked something. "Get a real criminal defense attorney."

After the phone call, she was escorted to the same tiny interrogation room. Again she was given coffee. This time she drank it, knowing she needed to be fully alert for whatever happened next.

When her lawyer, Jerry Whaland, showed up, she immediately fell in love because he brought her two bagels with cream cheese. Unlike most people, she did not lose her appetite in the face of a crisis. She just got hungrier. She wolfed down both bagels.

Heath did not interrogate her, which surprised her. Wasn't this his case? Instead she got the boss man himself, the much maligned Supervisory Special Agent Fleming Ketcher. She recognized him as the man who'd been in charge at her loft.

Brenna rode out the interrogation pretty well. Since she had nothing to hide, she didn't have to watch her words. She could just be honest, which she was good at.

"Why don't you give me a lie-detector test?" she asked brightly while her lawyer shook his head frantically.

"You don't want to do that, Brenna," Jerry said. "Lie detectors are notably unreliable. You could get a false positive simply because you're nervous."

"I don't care. I want one. I'm Marvin's victim, not his

co-conspirator. Why don't you talk to some of his other victims? You'll find out how sneaky Marvin is."

"We did talk to one of his other 'victims.' A Michelle Bernard?"

"Who? Oh, Shelly." The bank teller in Faring, Louisiana.

"He tried to enlist her in his schemes and succeeded, at least for a while. Then there was Ardith Smelter."

Shoot. Her own argument turned against her.

"You're not talking to the right victims," Brenna said. "What about Cindy Rheems and Sonya Patterson?"

"Not reliable. They just spent two days with you. You could have coached them."

This was ridiculous. No matter what she said, they wouldn't believe her, unless she confessed. She looked at Jerry, who'd tried to call a halt to the interrogation several times when Ketcher kept covering the same territory over and over. He gave her an encouraging look. Clearly he wanted her to shut up. She was just making matters worse.

"Okay, I'm done," she said. "I don't have anything further to add."

"You're done when I say you're done," Ketcher shot back. "What about Agent Packer?"

"What about him?"

"How does he figure into this?"

"You should know better than me." Her answer wasn't what he expected. He gave her a perplexed look, then pressed his thin lips together in dissatisfaction.

"I wasn't the one sleeping with him," he said finally.

Brenna didn't bother responding. If they continued this line of questioning, she would simply not answer, she decided. If they wanted to know prurient details, they could get them from Heath.

"Look," Ketcher said in a more reasoning tone, "there's no point in your lying about it. Packer has told us everything you told him. He has a great deal of it on tape."

"Tape?"

"In addition to your phone being wiretapped, he taped many of your personal conversations. Your continued denials will only make you look more guilty in a courtroom."

"If he said that, then he's a scum-sucking liar! I've never confessed to anything, not to Heath and not to anyone. I've been trying to tell you, that conversation with Marvin was a setup. A sting!"

The attorney put a restraining hand on her arm, but she shook it off.

"Brenna, hold it together," he warned.

She took a couple of deep breaths, knowing that losing her temper would not serve her. "If Heath said I confessed to something, he's lying. I didn't do anything, I haven't confessed to anything, I won't confess to anything except a bad habit of falling in love with grossly inappropriate men."

"Oh? Love? Is that what you call it?" Ketcher said with a sneer.

"Yes," she answered without hesitation. "I'm pitifully naive, eternally optimistic, no matter how many men disappoint me. And they do. I'm an easy target because I'm a hopelessly sappy romantic. Last I checked, that wasn't a crime."

Ketcher tried a few more tricks. He promised her a lighter sentence if she would confess and turn state's evidence against Marvin. But they couldn't crack her—there was nothing to crack. Strangely, the longer Ketcher wailed on her, the easier it became to deflect his attacks.

Ketcher finally gave up.

Agent Patty ferried Brenna through the next few grueling hours, steadfastly refusing to answer Brenna's questions about Heath. Heath had probably requested to be taken off her case, she reasoned. He knew exactly what she would put him through. The way she'd stared at him on the trip from New Orleans was just a tiny sample of the guilt she would pile on him now.

Patty took her to the U.S. Marshals Office, where she was processed all over again. Then she was taken before a judge at the county courthouse, who asked her if she understood the charges against her. She said she did, resisting the urge to editorialize. Jerry had warned her her smart mouth would get her into trouble if she didn't say what he told her to say.

Almost immediately after the first hearing, she went before another judge, who set her bail at an untenable one million dollars—because of her rich family, Jerry explained, and because they considered her a flight risk. Her parents, bless their hearts, were there to support her. They would have to come up with some cash to bail her out, but they promised it wasn't a problem, it would just take a bit of time.

After that she was driven to the Lew Sterritt Justice Center, which housed the Dallas County Jail. There, she was put through the humiliating experience of waiting in a holding tank with a bunch of prostitutes and junkies who eyed her with undisguised malevolence. Then she had to undress before a female guard-type person and surrender her own clothes. She was given an ill-fitting prison jumpsuit and taken to a different cell, with two bunks and a bathroom that afforded an appalling lack of privacy. She was given a comb, toothbrush and toothpaste, soap and shampoo. Clearly they thought she would be here awhile.

Brenna quickly made up the bed with the starchy sheets she'd been given, but she couldn't make herself sit on it, much less lie down.

How had she ended up like this? In a few short hours, she'd gone from the bliss of making love to her dream man to a hard-as-a-rock metal bunk in a five-by-eight cell—alone, betrayed, falsely accused.

She didn't often give in to tears, but her situation overwhelmed her. Exhausted, sore from the hours of hunching over her workbench, she let the tears come. She didn't even try to stop them. She just let her eyes leak and drip down her face onto the ugly gray jumpsuit.

IN THE INTERROGATION ROOM next door to the one Brenna in which had spent so many hours, Heath was faring better. He could only laugh and shake his head when Ketcher told him Brenna had confessed and implicated him. "You could break out the hot lights and rubber hoses, and Brenna wouldn't confess to something she hadn't done," he said, utterly sure of the woman he'd come to know so well over the past couple of weeks.

He freely admitted to Ketcher and two agents from Internal Affairs that he'd shown bad judgment in getting emotionally and sexually involved with a suspect. He had, after all, made love to her in New Orleans, before he'd been told she was in the clear. He fully expected to be relieved of his duties. But he hadn't perpetrated any crimes.

"Testify against her, and it'll all go away," Ketcher said in a way that was supposed to be enticing.

"You're out of your ever-lovin' mind."

Heath did manage one victory. At his insistence, Brenna's loft was searched, and all the receipts uncovered proved she'd recently purchased the precious metals and gemstones to create the new cache of jewelry. So the insurance-fraud angle wasn't going to fly.

But that taped conversation with Marvin wasn't going to disappear. On the surface it did look bad.

But it wasn't Heath's voice on the tape. In the end, they really had no proof he was involved, and they had to let him go.

Heath had only one thing left to do before he exited the interrogation room. He reached into his jeans pocket, withdrew his FBI credentials, and laid them on the table. They'd already confiscated his gun.

"I'll save you the trouble of suspending me and going through all the paperwork. I quit."

Ketcher just shook his head. "You almost threw your career away by protecting Christine. Didn't you learn anything?"

The question didn't even make Heath angry. It just confirmed he'd made the right decision. "First, I never protected Christine. I did not know of her criminal activities until her arrest, after which I cooperated fully and disclosed everything. But you know that, you just choose not to believe it.

"Second, it wasn't much of a career. I joined the FBI with the idealistic notion that I would help bring criminals to justice. But I spent most of my time catering to colossal egos, playing office politics and filling out paperwork. The Bureau did nothing but cause me to doubt my own instincts and turn me into a yes-man. And if I never wear another tie, it'll be too soon."

Ketcher did not have a snappy comeback, and Heath exited before the SSA found his tongue.

In the FBI Field Office parking lot, Heath breathed the air as a free man and allowed himself to experience relief.

Then he turned to more practical matters. His first order of business was to find out what had happened to Brenna. He could not trust anything Ketcher had told him.

A few inquiries turned up the fact that not only had she been arrested and interrogated, she'd been arraigned, bail set, and she'd been processed into Lew Sterritt. He couldn't even imagine how terrified she must be. He could remember Christine's frightened eyes when he'd been to visit her after her arrest, her hysterical pleas for him to bail her out, get a lawyer, make it all go away. He hadn't been able to help her. Thanks to the precarious financial situation she herself had put him in, he hadn't been able to come up with the collateral needed by a bail bondsman or the retainer for an attorney.

This was a different situation, he reminded himself. Brenna was innocent, he had money—some, anyway—and he would move mountains to help her.

When he tried to get in to see her, he discovered her parents were already there. They regarded him with overt suspicion and offered barely polite greetings.

"Have you talked to her?" he asked anxiously.

"We have everything under control," Mr. Thompson said coolly. "They're processing her release now." He looked irritated, as if Heath were a troublesome bug.

But Francine Thompson stepped within inches of Heath, putting her face in his, which she could do because she was almost as tall as he was. "You have some nerve," she hissed, "showing up here all concerned when it's your fault she's in jail in the first place."

This was so categorically wrong that Heath had a hard time defending it. Where did he start? But before he could even begin, Mrs. Thompson continued her diatribe.

"I would suggest you clear out of here before Brenna

shows up. She was in a foul temper when she was arrested, and several hours in jail haven't improved it any."

"If I could just explain—"

"Explain how you were just doing your job?" The slightly shrill voice that had interrupted him was not Mrs. Thompson's, but from Brenna herself. It had taken Heath a moment to recognize it because he'd never heard quite that level of loathing in her voice before. The double doors she'd just come through were still vibrating slightly, but Heath and her parents had been so engrossed they hadn't been aware of her arrival.

"That's not what I would have said."

"And I suppose you know nothing about that tape recorder set up in the empty loft next to mine?"

"I had no clue it was there. Brenna, you have to believe me."

But apparently she didn't. And why would she? He'd deceived her in the past. No reason she should trust him now. No reason at all.

Brenna swept past him, haughty as a queen, and her parents started to follow. "Wait," Heath called to her. "I have something important to tell you."

"I don't want to hear your apologies."

"I just wanted to tell you that your jewelry is waiting for you at the FBI Field Office."

She stopped. "You took my jewelry?"

"*I* didn't." Apparently Brenna hadn't been told of his arrest, which didn't surprise him. Ketcher had lied to both of them.

In her current mood, she wasn't going to stand idly by and listen to some long-winded explanation. "You still have time to make the plane to New York," he said. "I can go by your place and pack up the display cases and the

sign. You go pick up the jewelry and meet me at the airport."

"Are you crazy?" But Brenna's eyes lit up with a wild
kind of hope. "I just got out on bail. I can't just leave Dallas…can I?"

"I signed the bond agreement," her father said. "All I
promised was that you'd show for your preliminary hearing in two weeks."

"So you think I should do what *he* says?" She pointed
at Heath and curled her lip as if he were the Creature from
the Black Lagoon.

Brenna's mother spoke up. "Baby, I don't think you
should blow this chance. You might not get another. I did
some reading up on this IJC show. I had no idea it was such
a big deal. Fergie might be there, for heaven's sake. And
Gwyneth Paltrow!"

Chapter Fourteen

As surprised and hurt as Brenna was over Heath's betrayal, she was almost as shocked by her parents suddenly turning into her staunch supporters, her cheerleaders. For years they'd referred to her jewelry making as Brenna's "little hobby." What had hurt most was her father's refusal to even consider carrying her jewelry line in his store. But now here they were, rushing around as if getting her on that plane to New York was the most important thing in the world.

Brenna was nearly sick to her stomach as she walked into the FBI Field Office. She had this wild, paranoid fantasy that they would take one look at her and decide she ought to be locked up again, never mind that her parents had paid her bond. Or they would be able to see, just by looking at her, that she was planning to board a plane out of state and they would forbid it.

"Let me do the talking," her father said, his mind apparently moving along the same paths. He was afraid she would blurt out something that would get her into trouble.

But once they heard Marcus Thompson's name, the process was fairly streamlined. It surprised her that the FBI would hand over thousands of dollars worth of jewelry to her, a suspected thief. But it *was* her jewelry.

They gave it to her in a paper sack. She opened the sack right there in the FBI building, counting the pieces, checking each one for damage. The evidence people had considerately placed each one in a small plastic bag.

"Those are beautiful," her mother said, with something akin to wonder in her voice. "You made these?"

"I did," Brenna said, feeling suddenly proud of herself.

"Which one do you think Fergie will buy?"

"Mom, I doubt Fergie will give me a second look. She probably already has her favorite designers."

"Don't shortchange yourself, Brenna," Francine lectured. "I didn't raise any shrinking violets. You *make* them notice you."

Brenna almost laughed. This from the mother who'd constantly told her to be humble and not draw attention to herself because it was vulgar.

When she arrived at the airport, she asked her parents to drop her off at the ticketing area. She wanted to be alone when she encountered Heath again.

"Before you go, let me give you something," her father said. He popped the trunk of his Mercedes, then got out and walked around to the back. Brenna turned around and watched him, curious. When he returned, he had his Cordovan leather briefcase, the one her mother had had specially made for him a few years back. She expected him to extract something out of the briefcase, but instead he handed the whole case to her. "You can't try to board a plane with a paper sack full of jewelry. They'll think you just robbed a jewelry store."

"Marcus," Francine said, "don't even joke about something like that."

But he was right, Brenna realized. She emptied the sack into the briefcase.

"There's also a little cash in there," her father whispered. "You can't go to New York broke."

She got out and hugged both her parents. Even if this jewelry show was a fiasco, even if they laughed her out of that fancy hotel and sent her running back to Dallas with her tail between her legs, she could handle it, knowing her parents didn't hate her. She promised herself that when she returned to Dallas, she would have a good long talk with them—with her brothers and sisters, too. Maybe at Thanksgiving.

Then she was waving goodbye, clutching the briefcase, wishing she could handcuff it to her wrist, except that she really never wanted to see a pair of handcuffs again.

When she got to the ticketing area for her airline, she searched the milling crowd for Heath, yearning to see him yet wishing she could avoid it, too. Though she hurt down to her marrow every time she thought about how he'd tried to use her vulnerability with men to trap her, she still loved him. She couldn't help it; she just did.

Honesty compelled her to admit that he had not deliberately seduced her. He had tried to avoid that. She'd been the one to drag him to bed. She'd been the one to take advantage of him in New Orleans when he'd been off balance from the unexpectedly potent Hurricanes. And there were some things he couldn't fake, no matter how talented a trickster he was.

Her face glowed warm at the memory of last night's lovemaking. Surely he felt something for her. He'd been playing a part, the part of her confidant, but she couldn't believe it was all play-acting.

Or maybe she could. She had to stop being such a complete idiot when it came to men.

Funny, she'd never felt sad about Marvin when she'd

discovered his crimes. She'd believed herself in love, but since that horrible morning she'd awakened alone and destitute, she'd felt nothing but searing anger toward Marvin. She'd not wasted even a moment fantasizing how things might have turned out differently.

But with Heath…maybe that meant she really loved him. Real, adult, grown-up love. Damn, she was going to start sniffling in a minute if she didn't pull herself together.

She did pause to wonder why he was going to so much trouble to ensure she and her jewelry made it to New York.

She was starting to get anxious when finally she saw him coming from the elevator. He had a rolling cart with her suitcase and the two packing crates she used for her display cases. He looked rattled—and gorgeous, all rumpled in his jeans and T-shirt. He hadn't shaved all day, and he looked more like a dashing fugitive than law enforcement.

She schooled her face to neutrality. "I see you made it."

He glanced at his watch. "Not much time to spare. Any trouble getting the jewelry?"

"Surprisingly none." They got in line.

"Here, you'll need this." He opened the front zipper compartment on her suitcase and pulled out her small leather purse, which had her plane ticket, her ID and her maxed-out credit card. Thank goodness. She found her keys, too.

Curious about what all he'd packed for her, she went down on one knee and dug through the contents. She was surprised at how thorough he'd been—cosmetics, toiletries, all here. Panties, bras—her face flushed again—jeans, a couple of knit tops and—the red dress. Stockings. Her red killer heels. And, way at the bottom, jumbled into a plastic sandwich bag, her silver charms. She reached up and touched her ear, realizing for the first time all day that she wasn't wearing her signature jewelry. She felt naked.

She looked up to find him studying her, one corner of his mouth quirked up in amusement. He'd been waiting for her to find the charms, like watching a child hunt for Easter eggs.

"Looks like you thought of everything." She put on the various earrings, necklaces, rings and bracelets and, for the first time since she'd awakened this morning, began to feel more like herself and less like Dorothy swept away by the tornado. As soon as they got through this obnoxious line and to the gate area, she would go to the ladies' room and change clothes. Her sweatpants and the jail-issue flip-flops—which were only slightly less weird than her fuzzy slippers would have been—earned her quite a few strange stares. Air travelers dressed casually these days, but usually not quite to this degree.

When they were finally called to a ticket agent, Heath dragged their stuff over, put the first crate on the scale, then said, "Two to LaGuardia, Heath Packer and Brenna Thompson." He handed over his driver's license, then held out his hand for Brenna's.

Brenna just stood there, frozen. His duffel bag was sitting there next to her black suitcase. How had she missed seeing it before? "You're going to New York with me?"

"That's my plan."

"Really?" The ticket agent flashed her an annoying glance, so she dug out her license and handed it to Heath, who passed it to the agent. "Why?"

"How about looking for Marvin?"

How was she going to stand it? He still had such power over her. She had a terrible time holding on to being mad at him after he'd helped her so much. No matter how many times she reminded herself that he'd had a hidden agenda, that he'd been trying to entrap her, she couldn't stay mad. And if she had to spend three hours with him, he would figure it out and she would be at his mercy.

Then something occurred to her. "Ohhhh, I get it. You're still under orders to watch me." Of *course* he was. She congratulated herself for figuring it out. For once, she wasn't falling for his baloney.

"No, that's not it."

She whispered, so the ticket agent couldn't hear, "Do you check your gun through? Or do you wear it on the plane?" But she didn't see his shoulder holster, and there was no way he could pack heat in the snug jeans and T-shirt he wore.

"I'm not traveling with a gun."

"Will they issue you a new one when you get to New York?" She was curious how it all worked. With all the security regulations, maybe even law enforcement couldn't take their guns on planes.

"I'll explain later," he said as he collected their boarding passes. At least they would have something neutral to talk about on the plane.

Getting through security with the jewelry was a bit challenging, and Heath was no help. He stood to the side, letting her explain and explain about the jewelry show. They'd finally let her through, seeing as it wasn't a crime to carry an obscene amount of jewelry onto a plane.

"You could have helped," she groused as they walked to the gate.

"Me? How?"

"You could have flashed your badge."

He said nothing, but he looked pained, as if he'd just

swallowed worms. Her heart softened slightly, and she mentally kicked herself. How could she possibly be so dim, so easily manipulated?

"I need to change clothes," she said abruptly. "Will you watch my briefcase?" She figured whatever else Heath was, he wasn't a thief.

He nodded. "I'll be at the gate."

Brenna felt five hundred times better after changing into her favorite black jeans and a thin, neon pink knit shirt. She washed her face and brushed her teeth, then put on a lot of makeup. She didn't have any hair product—Heath had overlooked that. But she dampened her hair, then kneeled under the hand dryer and fluffed it up until it was a wild tangle of white-blond spikes with dark roots. Very tacky, very obvious, very Brenna.

That slightly mellowed version of herself she'd become under Heath's influence was conspicuously absent. Good. She needed all her armor to ward off her unhealthy affection for a man who was so, so wrong for her. She gave her head a shake, letting her earrings tinkle musically, and felt ready to face him again.

She found him at the gate, where he said he'd be, holding her briefcase in his lap, one hand closed securely over the handle.

She sat down next to him, then decided that was too close and moved one chair away. She was afraid she still might smell like prison antiseptic. She looked forward to bathing for real.

"Are you hungry?" he asked.

"Do you have a clue what passes for food in jail? It looked like it might have been chicken, but I couldn't swear to it, with some sort of congealed, jellylike stuff on it that I guess was supposed to be sauce or gravy. Canned, salty green beans, and a hunk of something they called cobbler that was cold as January asphalt and about as hard."

Heath laughed. "I'll take that as a yes. There's a little bar and grill down the way."

She wanted to say no. She could last until she got her airplane dinner. But then she remembered the quality of the last airplane dinner she'd eaten and nodded her agreement.

They sat at the bar and shared a plate of nachos and, to Brenna's surprise, Heath ordered a beer.

"Drinking on duty? Didn't you learn your lesson?"

"I'm not on duty. As a matter of fact, I'm unemployed. I don't know whether to celebrate or mourn the fact, but either way, beer seems appropriate." The bartender set a frosty mug in front of Heath, and he picked it up, offered a silent toast and downed a few swallows. "That's why I'm not traveling with a gun, and that's why I couldn't help you out at the security checkpoint. I don't have the authority to write a parking ticket, much less override airport security."

Brenna breathed in sharply. What new game was this? Deciding she'd been a sap for the last time, she shook her head. "Oh, nice try. Am I supposed to sympathize? Maybe get a little drunk and spill my guts, now that you're *unemployed?* Right."

Heath shrugged, but a slight tic in his left eye indicated he wasn't as cavalier as he appeared. "Maybe it would be better if we just didn't talk. I'll get you to the show like I said I would. Then you'll never have to see me again."

That was a depressing thought. Heath Packer had begun to feel like a permanent fixture in her life. As mad as she was at him, the thought of his disappearing forever was unbearably sad. Not even a heaping plate of nachos dripping with melted cheese and a mountain of jalapeño peppers could cheer her. She managed to nibble at them, focusing her gaze firmly on the TV set, which was broadcasting highlights from some hockey game.

"You're not eating," Heath said.

"I thought we weren't talking."

"When you don't eat, I get worried."

"I'm not in the mood to get teased about my unladylike appetite." She fished a twenty out of the briefcase from the stash her father had given her, threw it on the bar, hopped down from her stool and stalked out. She'd almost rather be back in jail than enduring this.

WELL, THAT HAD GONE OVER like the Hindenburg. Heath drained his beer and returned to the gate himself. Brenna had wedged herself between two families with children so there was no place nearby for him to sit. She had her face buried in a newspaper.

With a sigh he found a chair where he could keep an eye on her. Angry or not, she had a very valuable briefcase in her possession. He could at least ensure that she and the jewelry got to New York unscathed.

She boarded ahead of him. When he got to his seat, he discovered a woman in her sixties sitting where Brenna should have been sitting. "Are you sure you have the right seat?" he asked the strange woman politely.

She gave him a nasty look. "Your girlfriend traded with me. She said I was to be as mean as possible to you, and if I don't want my peanuts, I'm to give them to her, not you."

Heath laughed. If Brenna was showing her sense of humor, all was not lost. "Did she really say she was my girlfriend?" Heath asked.

"Uh, no, I just gathered. She's not?" the woman asked with interest.

Heath took the seat beside her. "Not at the moment. But I'm working on it."

"Oh." The woman looked as if she wanted to hear more but was too polite to pry.

"You wouldn't believe me if I told you," he said.

Though he caught glimpses of Brenna during the flight, he didn't reunite with her until they reached the baggage claim at LaGuardia. A skycap helped them manhandle the suitcases and crates outside to the line of taxis. Brenna tipped the man exorbitantly.

"Are you back to spending the money Cindy gave you?" he asked.

"No. I returned that to her. I didn't feel right about keeping it. But my dad gave me some money." She flashed him an annoyed look. "I thought we weren't talking."

"Right." That was his idea, after all, to not talk. But he found he couldn't stay mad at Brenna. Given her history, she had a right to doubt everything he or any man said to her. He would like to think that after what they shared—last night? Was it only last night? Anyway, she should at least give him the benefit of the doubt. He'd told her everything last night—all about Christine, and the challenges he'd been facing trying to get his colleagues to trust him again. Couldn't she see that he'd long since stopped playing games with her?

Then again, those esteemed former colleagues apparently had done everything they could to make it appear he had double-crossed her.

"I hope you have a room somewhere," Brenna said cheerfully as they climbed into the cab. "You're not staying in mine."

"You have one?"

"I reserved one a long time ago, before all the trouble started. At the Howard Johnson's."

"I got a room at the Crystalle. That's where the IJC show is, right?"

She nodded, and for an instant, Brenna's face reflected longing. Then she schooled her features. "Must be nice to travel on the federal government's dime. I couldn't afford the Crystalle."

"It's on my dime. I just thought…never mind." At the time he'd thought it would be a nice treat. Okay, he'd had hopes of seducing Brenna with luxury and room service and a Jacuzzi tub. The only time during their acquaintance they'd had any chance to relax or have fun was the night they went out on the town in New Orleans—the Night of the Hurricanes, as he'd come to think of it.

Now he would be rattling around the big, plush room all alone.

He helped her unload at the HoJo's—she wasn't too proud to accept his muscle, since she probably would have had to tip the cabbie a fortune to get him to drag those crates to her room.

"What time do you need me here in the morning?" he asked.

"Normally I would tell you to buzz off, that I don't need your help. But since I know it's your job to stick to me like glue, you'll be hanging around anyway. I might as well take advantage."

"My muscles are yours for the duration."

"Just don't get any ideas about that love muscle. Be here at six. Bring coffee." With that, she slammed the motel room door in his face.

Chapter Fifteen

The elevators at the swanky Hotel Crystalle were crowded as dozens of anxiety-ridden gem dealers and designers fought to get their carts, bags and boxes on board. As tempers flared, the hotel's event manager, a fussy little man with a thin mustache, fluttered around apologizing for the elevator situation. Because of some sort of electrical snafu, four of the hotel's eight elevators were out of order.

Brenna endured an elbow in her back and a cart wheel rolling over her toe before she finally emerged onto the top floor. Then all discomforts were forgotten as she gaped.

The Moonlight Ballroom was like nothing Brenna had ever seen before. She'd heard about it, of course. New York debutantes fought to have their weddings here. Events had to be booked sometimes years in advance.

Now Brenna understood why. The ceiling was so high no ladder could possibly reach it. It reminded her of a cathedral. She wondered how they ever changed a lightbulb. Then she realized she couldn't even see any lightbulbs. The indirect lighting was so cleverly hidden that the room seemed to glow of its own accord.

The walls were padded silk, the trim a rich mahogany. As she and Heath pushed and pulled a cart with all her display items, the wheels repeatedly snagged in navy blue carpet so thick a herd of antelope could hide in it.

They found Brenna's booth, Number 25. It was at the end of a row, as far from the ballroom entrance as possible and close to an alcove that led to the restrooms.

"Well, at least people will have to pass you on the way to the bathroom," Heath said cheerfully.

Brenna did not know what to make of him. He'd shown up at precisely six with a large coffee already doctored with plenty of cream and sugar, the way she liked it. He'd been relentlessly helpful as they'd lifted and toted crates and bags in and out of taxi trunks and elevators, and she'd decided being surly toward him took too much mental energy, so she'd been properly grateful, even nice.

When she was engrossed in assembling the tall round display case, he disappeared for a while. She figured he'd grown tired of the tedium and her nervous anxiety, which was building by the minute, but he returned before too long with a plate of the most delectable fruit, cheese and toasted bagels she'd ever seen.

"Where did you get these?"

"There's a buffet table set up at the other end of the room for exhibitors."

"Wow." She'd never been to a trade show where they actually fed the exhibitors. Then again, the fee to be included in this show had been about five times the norm, so the organizers could probably afford to be generous.

She stopped working long enough to eat, knowing that erratic blood sugar was at least partly responsible for her jumpy stress. She should be in ecstasy. She'd longed to be included in an event like this for years, where she could really strut her stuff. Maybe she would bomb; she was a brand-new designer in these people's eyes, not an insider.

There was no cachet attached to her name. But all it took was for her jewelry to catch the eye of just one influential buyer. Just one.

She cleaned the plate and felt better. More optimistic.

Heath hung her sign at the back of her small booth as she draped blue-gray velvet in her cases and lovingly arranged and rearranged her cases. A number of people she guessed were other exhibitors walked casually by her booth, eyeing her wares from the corners of their eyes. Absolutely none stopped to say hi, to welcome her as the new kid on the block, or to compliment her work.

This was nothing like the friendly flea markets and craft shows she was used to. It was intimidating.

"They see you as a competitive threat," Heath said.

"I think they just see me as that hick upstart from Dallas."

"No. If they felt sorry for you, they'd be nicer."

"You think? Or are you just trying to make me feel better?"

"I think. I've been watching people after they walk away. They're whispering about you and looking worried. They're not laughing behind your back."

Brenna still felt like the new kid in school with the homemade dress and mismatched socks. Not that she'd ever been a kid like that, but she had a good imagination.

Once she got the booth arranged and draped to her satisfaction, she stood out in the center of the room to admire it from a distance. Then she looked at some of the other exhibitor's spaces, and what optimism she had fled straight out the window. The other booths—if you could call them that—looked like the interiors of posh jewelry stores, complete with oriental rugs and indirect lighting. By comparison, her space looked as if it belonged at the Podunk County Fair.

It was the jewelry that mattered, she told herself over and over.

She'd been so busy, she hadn't even noticed until now the buffet table being set up in the center of the ballroom for the guests, who would be arriving soon. Calling it a "table" was understating the situation; it was a buffet mountain, multileveled, with a champagne fountain and glaciers of stacked crystal glasses, everything draped in yards and yards of royal blue silk and garlands of orchids, white roses and tiny white lights.

The crowning glory was the biggest ice sculpture she'd ever seen of—yes, a naked woman. She vaguely recognized it as a reproduction of some famous Roman statue—*Diana the Huntress,* she thought.

When she returned to her booth, which Heath was guarding, she found a list of last-minute instructions from the organizers. The buffet was for guests, not exhibitors. The exhibitors had their own refreshment room outside the ballroom and down a hall, where soft drinks and snacks would be provided.

No caviar and champagne for the hoi polloi, she thought with a grin.

"You'd better change your clothes," Heath said. "It's almost time."

Brenna's heart skipped a few beats as she grabbed her clothes and headed for the ladies' room, where other women were dressing and primping and gossiping. Conversation stopped when she entered, and all eyes were briefly on her before the other women suddenly found buttons that had to be fastened and items that had to be dug for in purses and cosmetic cases.

Brenna wiggled into her red dress, which thankfully was not too wrinkled, then went to work on her makeup.

She overheard someone talking about the critics who would be here, searching for flaws and weaknesses. The annual display of ostentation for the rich and famous was a favorite target for journalists.

They were bound to target her, she thought in despair. The new kid on the block was always more closely scrutinized. Maybe she should just pack up and go home now.

Brenna returned to her booth, almost shaking. Critics! A horror she'd never considered. She wanted to vent to Heath, whom she knew would at least make sympathetic noises. But he disappeared to change his own clothes.

Brenna drank some bottled water—she didn't need any more caffeine—and waited. She checked and rechecked that she had everything she needed. Her cash box in a locked drawer, just in case anyone actually wanted to pay in cash, which she doubted. Her credit card machine. The organizers had told her she didn't need to bother with Chek-Tronic—all of the guests would be "financially pre-qualified." Business cards. Bags for the jewelry she sold. Jeweler's loupe and polishing cloths. Hand cream, which did little to help her work-roughened hands, but at least it smelled nice.

Heath returned, looking much as she'd seen him when they first met, in his FBI suit. Only, the bulge from the shoulder holster was missing. He really wasn't carrying a weapon, which surprised her.

"You look nice," she said. "You don't actually think you'll be making an arrest here, do you?"

"As I've explained," Heath said with false cheerfulness, "I won't be making any arrests ever again. I dressed in my Sunday best solely to be a good reflection on you."

To her immense irritation, she wanted to believe him. "But why?"

"Sometimes you are really dense." He arranged his chair in a back corner of the booth, allowing her center stage.

Dense? Yes, she could be slow-witted about any number of things. Like assessing people. Judging their characters.

Or had she been so wrong about Heath? She was really confused about him. Kind and generous lover, or conniving law enforcement agent who was so set on restoring his reputation that he would manufacture evidence?

Heath busied himself straightening her sign and adjusting the booth's draping like some fussy interior decorator. She realized he really did care what sort of impression she made.

She got up, took two steps and was standing inches from him. "Explain it to me. How am I dense?"

He stopped what he was doing and looked at her, really looked at her, and she saw something in his eyes that stopped her short. Uncertainty. He was as uncertain as her sixth-grade boyfriend when he first asked her to go bike riding with him.

"For gosh sake, just spit it out," she said.

"Okay. I love you, Brenna. How could you not see it? It must be oozing from my pores."

All the air whooshed out of Brenna's lungs. Even if she'd had a reply handy, which she didn't, she didn't get the chance to say anything. It was ten o'clock. The doors were opening. The guests had arrived. And Heath had said the one thing that would ensure she would be a babbling idiot in front of her customers.

"We're not done here," she said, shaking her finger at him.

"I hope not," he murmured with a faint smile.

The customers didn't flock in the way they did at regular trade shows. The richest of the rich didn't stand in line. They drifted in in twos and threes, mostly women but a few men, dressed in the most incredibly beautiful clothes, sporting Italian leather boots and tiny purses, probably enough to hold a credit card and a lipstick.

"Is that…is that…" She couldn't even utter the name of the A-list movie star who was strolling down the line of exhibitors.

"I think it is," Heath said, seeming unimpressed.

A few of the guests had obvious bodyguards walking a few paces behind, their sharp eyes darting every which way, not at the jewelry but at the people, alert to any threat.

A group of men in turbans entered, conversing in a language Brenna couldn't identify. She heard others around her saying "prince" and "raja" in speculative whispers.

Even if she didn't sell a single thing, she thought, this experience was worth it. She might not ever be invited back, but this day would be etched in her memory forever.

Especially the part where Heath had said he loved her.

What was with that? Was he really so devoted to his job that he would feign falling in love with her? Did he still hold out hope that with just a bit more sincerity he could convince her he was on her side?

But he'd looked so hopeful when he'd said it. Scared but hopeful.

Stop it! She ordered herself. She was doing it again. How many times did she have to fall for a man's line before she realized they were all fat liars?

"Oh, look at these!" a voice squealed, and Brenna realized with some shock that a patron was actually looking at her case. She'd been pretty invisible up to that point.

The voice came from a teenage girl, maybe eighteen, who had the thin, toned body, perfectly highlighted hair and satin-smooth skin that seemed to be particular to the rich. Brenna was familiar enough with the look—her prep school had been full of girls like this. Only this girl had had breast enhancement.

She was with an older man, whom Brenna hoped to high heaven was her father.

"Brenna," the man said, reading her sign. Then he looked straight at Brenna. "Never heard of her."

"I'm Brenna Thompson," Brenna said smoothly, rising from her chair. "I'm new this year. This is my premiere collection." She'd thought of that last night. "Premiere collection" sounded impressive.

"Oh, Daddy," the girl cooed, "look at that purple stone."

"It's an amethyst, honey. They're a dime a dozen."

"But it's *purple*. I *love* purple."

Me, too, Brenna wanted to say, amused by the girl's enthusiasm.

"I'll try that one on," she said, pointing to the ring designated for Brenna's sister.

"Certainly. But I have to warn you, this piece is spoken for. Everything in this case has been sold," she fibbed. "But I can make another, to your exact specifications."

"You mean I couldn't take it home today?" the girl said, disappointed.

"Well, not that ring," Brenna said. "But the pieces in this case here are available."

The teenager yanked off the ring and went for the case, scanning the contents hungrily.

"Honey," the man said, "I thought you wanted a Cathy Waterman ring." Waterman was a well-known designer who was one of Brenna's idols.

"I can at least look at these others, can't I?" She tried on a garnet ring, then one with peridots in a leaf design. Neither of those were quite showy enough. Then she spotted a necklace featuring a huge blue topaz set in a bold swirl of platinum and tiny diamonds.

She tried it on. "I want this."

"I thought you wanted a ring," her father said.

"Changed my mind."

The father smiled indulgently. "Well, a girl turns sixteen only once." And he whipped out his credit card without even asking the price.

Brenna's hands shook as she processed the transaction. This girl preferred her jewelry to Cathy Waterman's. That was saying something. Then she actually looked at the credit card and realized she recognized the name. This guy was the CEO of a huge financial conglomerate.

A couple of other women had sidled up to Brenna's booth when they'd seen a sale taking place. One of them looked familiar. A soap star? They each tried on several items and lingered over the silver charms. Then they walked away without buying.

But other customers came right behind them. Things got so busy around her booth that Heath jumped in to help.

Listening to him with half an ear, Brenna was surprised to hear Heath speaking knowledgeably about the jewelry, the stones, the settings. He'd apparently been paying attention as she'd crafted the pieces. He complimented the women, not so lavishly that it looked like a sales schtick, but just enough to arouse their feminine instincts. An older woman and her twin sister placed orders for matching dragonfly scarf pins, but they wanted the tourmalines replaced with emeralds and sapphires.

The pair of women who'd walked away earlier returned.

"You know," said one, "this jewelry looks almost exactly like those pieces we looked at over there." She pointed one peach sculptured nail toward the opposite corner of the ballroom.

"Hey, you're right," said the other. "I remember that ring. Except it had a diamond rather than an amethyst."

Brenna shared a glance with Heath. Surely it didn't mean anything. These women probably didn't know what they were talking about.

"Oh, and remember that opal necklace we saw? Wasn't it just like that one there with the moonstone?" They gave Brenna a suspicious look, as if they thought she might have copied a famous designer's pieces.

That was all Brenna needed to hear. She was out of her chair. "Where did you see this other jewelry?" she demanded.

The women both took a step back. "Um, far corner. Jennifer something is the name of the jeweler."

Brenna stomped out of the booth.

"Brenna, wait," Heath called. "Maybe I should go."

But she didn't listen. She could almost feel the steam blasting out of her ears.

Marvin wouldn't dare! Would he? Would he show up here with her designs, knowing…then again, she'd told him she wouldn't be here.

As she rounded the buffet table at the other end of the ballroom, she slowed down and peeked around the corner. Jennifer Ruben's booth was hard to miss. She'd rented three spaces and had decked them out like a Turkish harem. There were tall, slender men in gray suits waiting on customers. And sitting in a padded chair like a queen was Jennifer, legendary jeweler to the stars. She was not a designer herself, but tended to have exclusive merchandising relationships with a half-dozen hot designers—always male designers—at any one time.

She was elegant, aristocratic—and blond.

Brenna assumed none of the salesmen would recognize her, and certainly Jennifer wouldn't know her from Adam. So she ambled up to the cases, which were bulging with an amazing array of ostentatious pieces.

Then she saw it, a small tabletop case sitting on a carved ebony stool. An engraved brass sign read, Designs by Todd Baker. And inside the case were at least a dozen of her jewelry pieces.

Adrenaline surged through Brenna. Her skin prickled, and her breath came in short gasps. She wanted to grab the display case and run with it! But she recognized that such behavior would only get her arrested. She also reasoned that Jennifer Ruben probably was a victim. She was about to make a graceful retreat when a tall man in a suit brushed past her and entered the Ruben exhibit. She at first thought he was another salesboy clone.

"Todd, where have you been?" Jennifer asked, sounding peeved. "You're missing all the excitement. I've sold three of your pieces already."

"That's incredible!"

Brenna froze. She knew that voice, though she'd never heard it injected with that note of boyish enthusiasm before.

The man turned before she could back away, and their gazes locked. Todd Baker, aka Marvin Carter, looked like a rabbit caught in a trap.

"You must be insane, to show your face here," Brenna said. It was the first thing that came to her mind.

He had the gall to give her a cocky smile. "I'm sorry, have we met?"

Jennifer gave Brenna a hard stare. "You aren't going to cause a scene, are you?"

She most certainly was. "Your hot new designer is a phony," Brenna practically spat. "He stole that jewelry from me."

"That's quite impossible," Jennifer said, flipping her long, blond hair over her shoulder.

Marvin took advantage of Brenna's momentary distraction and bolted from the booth.

"Oh, no, you don't!" Brenna cried, kicking off her heels and taking out after him. He was not going to get away this time. "Thief!" she called out. "Stop that man!"

But Marvin proved more slippery than a greased pig. When a knot of people blocked his way at the ballroom exit he did a quick U-turn. Brenna made a grab for him as he passed her, but she came up with only his jacket.

Undaunted, she changed direction and charged after him. He mowed down a well-known talk-show hostess and elbowed his way through the turbaned contingent like Br'er Rabbit through the briar patch.

But Brenna was fast, too, and small. She darted in and out of the shocked shoppers like a pinball.

She had him cornered near the end of the buffet table, but then he had the audacity to yank up the table's silk draping and duck underneath it. Grimly determined, Brenna followed. No matter what her loss of dignity, she was not going to let Marvin get away.

With her shorter arms and legs, she was lower to the ground and could crawl faster than he could. He headed down the length of the table. She crawled after him, banging her knees on table legs, running her stockings, getting a heinous case of carpet burn. But she almost had him. She grabbed his ankle. He gave a mighty jerk, and his shoe came off in her hand.

She tossed the shoe aside as he made a dive for the outside. Duckwalking, she followed. They came up in the middle of a terrified group of women, possibly an entire college sorority. Marvin pushed them aside like bowling pins.

"Sorry," Brenna murmured as she plunged after him. Cornered again, he vaulted over the buffet table, stepped his stockinged foot right in the middle of a cheese tray and, with a terrible crash, knocked over half the champagne-flute glacier.

Marvin's height gave him the advantage in jumping and climbing. Brenna tried to follow, but she slipped and ended up doing a belly flop into a mountain of caviar. *Mom,* she thought, *are you proud? They're sure noticing me now.* She scrambled to her feet, pulling herself up on the ice sculpture. To her horror, *Diana the Huntress*'s arm broke off in her hands.

Still clutching the ice arm, she leaped off the buffet table. A bevy of little old ladies had cornered Marvin. One was whapping him with her large alligator handbag and one was assaulting him with a spiked heel.

Still, he managed to get away.

But Brenna was within striking distance. Vengeance was close, so close. She did the only thing she could think of. She conked him on the head with the ice arm.

Chapter Sixteen

When Heath saw the commotion at the other end of the ballroom, he knew with a sinking feeling that Brenna was somehow involved.

Making sure Brenna's cases were all locked, he left the booth and headed toward the ruckus. But then he realized the ruckus was headed for him. He watched in amazement as a chase scene worthy of the *Keystone Kops* unfolded from one end of the Moonlight Ballroom to the other.

He took out after the man in the lead, whom he assumed was Marvin Carter. But his efforts were hampered at every turn as he tried to make his way through the crowded ballroom.

He caught sight of Marvin again when the wily man ducked under the table. Rather than following, which would be an exercise in futility given Heath's height and bulk, he waited to see where they'd come out.

When they did, they were far away from his grasp. He watched, stunned, as Marvin leaped across the buffet, Brenna in hot pursuit. He really could not believe it when Brenna dived into the caviar, then broke the arm off the ice sculpture.

Security guards were blocking both the main exit and

the fire escape, so Heath did not see how Marvin could escape now. When Heath reached the center of the melee, it was all over.

Marvin staggered after Brenna popped him with the ice arm, then fell to his knees as a group of uniformed hotel security guards, who looked decidedly ill equipped to handle this situation, converged on him.

"Stop right there, both of you," the guards' ringleader commanded.

"He's a thief. He's wanted by the FBI," Brenna hurriedly informed them. Then she looked over, saw Heath and smiled gratefully. "Heath, tell them. This is Special Agent Heath Packer. He's been tracking this man for weeks."

Heath really wished he hadn't resigned. He would love to have been able to step forward, flash his credentials and slap some handcuffs on Marvin.

Instead he said, "I'm a former special agent to the FBI. It's true, this is Marvin Carter, and he is wanted by the FBI. You can check with any FBI Field Office."

"What about her?" one of the guards asked, nodding toward Brenna.

She was still holding the ice arm, and she quickly set it down. But the guilty look on her face said it all. She realized the enormity of the damage she'd inflicted. The hotel and the International Jewelry Consortium would be perfectly within their rights to have her arrested. Then they'd look up her record in some computer, see that she was a theft suspect herself out on bond, and she'd never see daylight again.

She looked imploringly at Heath.

"She was trying to make a citizen's arrest. The perp stole from her, stole from her parents, then framed her for it. Cut her some slack."

He had no authority here, but to his relief, people were listening to him and nodding.

Then, incredibly, Marvin wiggled free from his security guard captors. They'd probably never collared a violent fugitive in their lives; it seemed a small matter for Marvin to poke one in the eyes, elbow some ribs, kick out a knee. Then he was gone.

Heath didn't hesitate. He gave chase, yelling "Stop!" and "Freeze!" in his best FBI voice. As if that would stop someone as desperate as Marvin obviously was. He'd never seen a criminal with more chutzpah—or more sheer athleticism. The guy could probably run a four-minute mile.

Marvin headed for the elevators. Two repairmen in gray jumpsuits were squatting by the door of one elevator. The doors were open, a halogen light illuminating the interior.

Marvin barreled toward it.

"Marvin, stop!" Heath yelled, horrified. The repairmen turned and added their shouts to Heath's. But Marvin didn't even slow down. He leaped over the two repairmen like a gazelle—into the open elevator shaft. There was a scream, then nothing.

Heath skidded to a stop just in time to grab Brenna, who'd been right behind him. He halted her trajectory inches before she would have jumped into the shaft right behind Marvin.

"Oh, my God!" She clung to Heath, looking terrified. "Oh, my God, there's no elevator there!"

"We tried to warn him," one of the repairmen said anxiously.

Heath and Brenna peered over the edge of the floor into the dark shaft. "We're on the twenty-third floor," she said breathlessly.

"But it's not that far down to where the elevator car is stuck," said the repairman. "Only three floors."

"Three floors," Heath repeated.

"Could he survive that?" Brenna asked anxiously. "What if we chased him to his death?"

Heath shook his head. "He couldn't possibly be alive."

"Oh, yeah?" said the repairman, shining the bright halogen lamp downward.

And there was Marvin, looking up at them, bruised and battered but, by some freak of nature, not seriously injured. He flashed his disarming smile, waved goodbye, then stepped out through the doors he'd apparently pried open.

Security guards swarmed around them, babbling on their radios, but Heath had a feeling it was hopeless. Marvin Carter had escaped—again.

He looked back at Brenna, dreading the defeat he anticipated seeing in her eyes. But what he saw took his breath away. She was smiling, her eyes shining. She threw her arms around him and planted a passionate kiss on his lips.

Not one to look a gift horse in the mouth, he returned the kiss enthusiastically. All that adrenaline pumping through their veins…

Gratitude for saving her life, perhaps, for preventing her from plunging to her death?

But when she broke the kiss, what she said was, "You really *did* quit the FBI. Heath, why?"

"It's about time you asked that. Explanations will have to wait, I'm afraid."

They waited for a long time. New York's finest arrived, along with an agent from the FBI Manhattan Field Office, and the aftermath went on for hours. Fortunately the FBI agent, a good-natured, round-faced man named Reeves, knew Heath, remembered something about him other than the fact his wife had been convicted of felony theft and fraud, and listened intently as Heath spun the story of Marvin Carter.

"A Picasso, huh?"

"I suggest we get a warrant to search his hotel room, pronto, before he finds a way to get there ahead of us and clean it out."

An outraged Jennifer Ruben informed them that Marvin had a room right there in the Crystalle. The FBI quickly got the warrant, and the manager let him in. Reeves let Heath and Brenna tag along for the search, though they had to wait out in the hall.

They'd lucked out; Marvin hadn't managed to slip back in and make off with his belongings. Reeves and another agent made a thorough search of the room. "Looks like we found something," Reeves called out. Moments later he appeared in the hallway with a mailing tube. "Found it in the back of a closet." He opened the tube and gently extracted a rolled-up oil painting.

Brenna gasped when she saw it. "That's it. That's my parents' Picasso."

THE HOTEL MADE NOISES about filing charges against Brenna for the damage, but when they realized she was the daughter of a multimillionaire department-store mogul who would probably pay for everything, they backed down. In fact, the disturbance had gotten everyone all excited, and sales at the IJC show boomed.

Brenna, however, could not face returning to her booth and putting on a happy face. Beside the fact that her dress was covered in caviar and brie cheese, her stockings torn and her shoes missing, she had cuts and bruises all over her body.

Heath gave her the key to his room on the seventeenth floor. "Go sit in the hot tub. I'll take care of everything here."

He didn't have to ask her twice. She was so mad about Marvin escaping, and so humiliated over diving into caviar and breaking off Diana's arm in front of all those rich and famous people, she couldn't even get excited about the fact that she'd sold a few of her pieces. As she trudged toward the elevator, enduring many curious stares and whispers, she suddenly remembered that Heath had said he loved her—and everything else paled by comparison.

Heath. She felt a small surge of optimism. He hadn't been lying to her. The implications were staggering. No, her sheer stupidity was staggering. How come she was such a gullible pushover ninety-nine percent of the time, yet the *one time* she should have trusted a man, she got all skeptical and suspicious?

Why hadn't she, this one time, followed her heart? More important, could he ever forgive her for being so horrible to him?

BRENNA TOOK a two-hour whirlpool bath with mountains of bubbles. Then, because she had no clean clothes, she put on one of Heath's shirts, which hung almost to her knees, and ordered room service. As she ate a cheeseburger, fries and a chocolate milkshake, she wondered where Heath was. How much time would it have taken to break down her booth and pack up her stuff? A couple of hours, maybe, working alone.

The phone rang at three, and she pounced on it. "Hello?"

"How are you holding up?"

"Heath, where are you?" Just the sound of his voice lifted her spirits.

"In the ballroom, still. I'll be tied up for a while. Order room service."

"Um, yeah, I'll do that. Thanks."

"You'll stay there till I finish up?"

"Where would I go? I have no clothes."

"I'll hurry."

Hmm, she thought after hanging up. That was interesting and mysterious.

She racked up enormous charges on the hotel room phone, calling Cindy and Sonya on a conference call and filling them in on the latest with Marvin.

"That guy has more lives than a cat!" Cindy declared. "How are *you* holding up?"

"Do you need anything?" Sonya asked. "I could fly to New York."

"I'll be fine," she assured them, thinking that Sonya sounded way too anxious to escape her situation in Houston, about which she was being decidedly cagey.

"What about Mr. Sexy FBI Man?" Cindy asked.

"I'll give a full report when I get back home." When she knew how the story would end.

An Adam Sandler movie lulled her to sleep, and she didn't stir until Heath returned to the room. She jerked awake at the sound of the lock clicking. It was dark, and she was disoriented for a few seconds until Heath flipped on a light.

He looked relieved to see her. "I should have come back sooner," he said. "But things got crazy."

She wasn't surprised. The aftermath of Marvin's capture and escape, then the recovery of the Picasso, had probably created a tangle of bureaucratic red tape.

"Sorry I made you handle it alone," she said. "I see you remembered my dad's briefcase."

"There's not much in it," he said, tossing it onto the bed.

Brenna's heart sank. "Don't tell me my jewelry got stolen on top of everything else."

"No. I sold it. Well, not the pieces for your family, but everything else."

"Excuse me?"

"I don't know how to break the news, but you have become a bona fide celebrity. Your brazen takedown of a jewel thief with nothing but your bare hands—well, and Diana's arm—then Marvin's plunge down an elevator shaft and the subsequent recovery of a stolen Picasso is the stuff legends are made of. The reporters couldn't get enough of it."

"But I haven't talked to any reporters!" she objected, feeling a little like Cinderella, transformed from waif to princess.

Heath grinned. "I know. You disappeared, which makes you all that much more intriguing. Every single person at the IJC show wanted a piece of you. Or rather, a piece of your jewelry. You sold out, and I took advance orders for dozens more items, and several more have declared they want you to design original, one-of-a-kind pieces just for them."

"What about the pieces Jennifer Ruben had?" she asked.

"Taken into evidence. You'll get them back."

Heath opened the briefcase. Credit card slips were packed inside so tightly that they sprang out at her like a jack-in-the-box. She fanned through them. Thousands and thousands of dollars. "I'm rich!"

"And you have enough work to keep you busy for a year."

"That's okay!"

"Seeing as you're a heroine and all, the hotel hastily dropped their complaints against you. If you'll come back tomorrow, you'll get the VIP treatment. And I imagine you'll get a bunch of press interviews out of it. CNN was there. They interviewed me, but clearly I was the consolation prize."

Brenna had no words, but heck, what did she need words for. She threw her arms around Heath's neck and kissed him. He tensed in surprise at first, then answered her sensual assault with enough heat to set the bedspread on fire.

They fell onto the bed and things started accelerating pretty quickly. Buttons came undone, zippers unzipped. But Brenna abruptly remembered something and pulled back, grabbing both of Heath's hands to still them.

"Wait. You have to tell me what happened—I mean, why you're not an FBI agent anymore."

"Now?" he asked, his voice a bit ragged.

"Yes, now." She scooted farther from him, pulling his shirt back over her bare shoulder.

He rolled over onto his back, staring up at the ceiling, and sighed. "After they arrested you, they arrested me," he said. "Then they interrogated me for several hours. They told me you'd confessed, that you'd implicated me. They wanted to charge me with obstruction of justice."

Brenna gasped. "You mean they just lied?"

"There's no law against lying during an interrogation, if you're the one doing the interrogating. Of course, I knew it was all bull, and since they had no evidence against me, they had to let me go."

"I believed everything that awful Agent Ketcher said about you." She looked at Heath as despair crept into her soul once again. "I must be the worst judge of character on the face of the earth."

"Brenna, come here." He held out his arms. She hesitated only a moment, then scooted over and settled against him, her head on his chest, his arms protectively around her. "It's one of the things I love most about you—the fact that you're open and honest about everything, and you expect others to be."

"But I didn't trust you, and you were the one person I should have believed in."

"I gave you all kinds of reasons not to trust me. I lied to you in New Orleans. I'm the one who got into your room first. I searched your suitcase without your permission. John-Michael McPhee covered for me, I'm not sure why. I lied about other things, too. I didn't tell you you were a suspect. I didn't even hint that I was under orders to arrest you and bring you back to Dallas."

"And the tap on my phone?"

"That was a complete surprise to me. Ketcher thought all along I was protecting you. He told me the case against you was closed, but he still had you under surveillance. You *and* me."

"Fleming Ketcher isn't a very nice man."

"No. And I don't want to end up just like him, which is why I turned in my badge." He caressed Brenna's hair. "You have the perfect right not to trust me. But I swear, Brenna, I'll never, ever lie to you again."

"Silly me, I believe you," she said without hesitation. He'd said it again—that he loved her—but she was still so shocked by that, she couldn't address it yet. She moved to safer topics. "So you quit? Are you sure that was the thing to do? When I go to trial, I might need an FBI agent on my side."

"They were going to fire me. It was inevitable. I saved them the trouble."

"I'm so sorry," she said, meaning it. "I feel responsible."

"Yeah, you are. You made me realize that the FBI isn't for me. I learned a lot working for the Bureau, but it's too structured for me. Too much bureaucracy, too much paperwork and red tape."

"So what will you do?"

He thought about it for a moment. "Could I be your kept man?"

Actually, that didn't sound like such a bad idea. She'd liked having him around in her loft while she worked, fixing her meals, cleaning for her, stepping and fetching. But she knew he was kidding. "C'mon, really."

"I'll open a private investigations agency," he said, and she could hear the excitement in his voice. "I'll rent the space next door to yours. We could knock out some walls, reconfigure a bit, and have the biggest, coolest multiuse space in the city. The Thompson-Packer Private Investigations Firm and Jeweler's Studio. Although maybe you don't want a partner."

The crazy thing was, she could picture it. "I want a partner."

"In everything?" He pushed himself up on one elbow so he could see her face. "Partners in everything?"

She reached up to stroke his face. "Everything."

THE THOMPSON FAMILY enjoyed the most raucous Thanksgiving in recent memory. Everyone was there, wanting to celebrate the fact that the charges against Brenna had been quietly dropped and the Picasso returned to its rightful place on the living room wall.

Brenna had decided she could not wait until Christmas

to give her family their presents, so she broke tradition and did it Thanksgiving evening. They thought she was being a bit odd, but they indulged her.

She gave them out one at a time, wanting to watch each of her siblings' faces, and those of her parents and her in-laws, nieces and nephews, as they opened the small, shiny boxes and saw the jewelry pieces she had created especially for each one of them.

Thanks to the national publicity, and her offer to buy back certain pieces Marvin had sold to unwary buyers, Brenna managed to recover all of the original pieces made from her grandmother's gemstones.

Helen, normally so dignified, squealed in delight when she saw the huge diamond ring. Her sister Anne, the lawyer, got an understated platinum stickpin to wear on her suit lapels, while her sister Patricia, who had mountains of long, luxuriant red hair, got a silver comb set with topaz. Her brother the doctor got a pair of gold, diamond-crusted cuff links, and her mother, the dragonfly scarf pin with sapphires and emeralds, inspired by the piece she'd seen in New Orleans. Her nieces all got silver charm bracelets with some starter charms—ballet shoes for the dancer, a little piano for the musician, and so on. She'd been at a loss for the boys, so she gave them each a CD and a promise that, the first time they had a girl they wanted to impress, she would make a piece of jewelry for them.

Even Annalisa, the housekeeper, got a pair of dangly amethyst earrings.

When Brenna was done passing out the goodies, she felt like a load had been lifted off her shoulders. She'd made things as right as she could make them.

"Grandma would be so proud of you," said Helen, Brenna's oldest sister, who was usually her loudest critic.

"We're all proud of you," her father said, admiring his gold tie tack, which had been fashioned in the shape of the sailboat he planned to buy when he retired. "Now I have something for you." He handed her an envelope.

Inside was a check with a lot of zeroes.

Her heart sank. He still thought she needed his charity. "Oh, Dad, thanks," she said, trying to sound sincere, "but I don't need any money."

"This isn't charity. It's a business transaction. I want Thompson-Lanier to be your exclusive retailer. I have a contract in my office for you to look over."

Everyone in her family smiled expectantly at her. They'd all been in on this surprise, she realized. They all thought she deserved it.

"Oh, Dad." She hugged her father. "You can be my exclusive retailer for free."

"Nonsense. If I wanted the privilege for free, I should have started carrying your jewelry before you were famous. Now I'm willing to pay for my lapse in judgment and foresight."

Brenna would have burst out crying, but the doorbell rang. It was Heath, she already knew. She'd invited him over for a light supper, after which they would take a cab to the airport. They were going to St. Louis tonight so she could meet his family.

Her relatives flocked around him as if he were a rock star. "You missed seeing us open Brenna's presents," said Patricia, sporting her new bejeweled comb.

"Ah, but there's one last present," Heath said, pulling a very small box from his pocket and handing it to Brenna. She looked at it suspiciously. She was the only one who was supposed to be giving gifts today. Her father's check had thrown her for a loop, but this…

"Are you just going to stand there?" Helen demanded. "Open it."

She did. Inside the tiny box was the most perfect oval diamond she'd ever seen, at least two carats.

"Is it bad luck for the bride to design her own engagement ring?" Heath asked innocently. She thought her heart was going to pop right out of her chest. Marriage? He actually wanted to marry her? She was shocked, overwhelmed, *thrilled*. But did he have to ask her to marry him here? In front of everybody?

Her family erupted in cheers and hugs and kisses and back slaps, apparently assuming this was not a surprise to Brenna, that she and Heath had already agreed to marry. Champagne appeared. Her mother cried in a way she had not done when Brenna announced her engagement to "Seneca."

Brenna went along with it, floating in a bubbly-induced haze, plotting what she would say when she got him alone. That wasn't until they were in the cab heading for the airport.

"Don't you think you could have asked me first? Privately?"

"I knew you couldn't say no in front of your family," he offered cheerfully, not in the least apologetic. Then he added, "You're not going to say it now, are you?"

"I wouldn't marry you if you were the last man on earth."

"Oh, Brenna, please. You are the worst liar on earth."

They kissed all the way to the airport.

* * * * *

Be sure to pick up the next BLOND JUSTICE *book, featuring Sonya Patterson, when* OUT-OF-TOWN BRIDE *debuts in December 2005!*

*Kaitlyn Rice knows the heartland of
the country—she herself lives in Kansas.
This is her first story in a miniseries entitled*
HEARTLAND SISTERS, *about the Blume girls,
Callie, Isabel and Josie. In this story,
Callie's estranged husband, Ethan,
shows up and is completely unaware that
the little boy who goes everywhere
with her is his. Callie has no plans to share
her secret with the man who once
abandoned her. So why can't she sign those
divorce papers releasing him—and her—
from their vows?*

Available October 2005

"Let's have a look, Miz Blume." The disaster worker's eyes met Callie's briefly before sinking to the stack of papers she'd just handed him.

She wasn't a Blume anymore. Callie frowned, but didn't bother to correct him. The man appeared to be around her age, twenty-nine, so he must remember her from her childhood here in Augusta, Kansas. That would explain the vague familiarity of his features, as well as the dull greeting he'd offered when she'd sat down across the table from him.

Local folks would probably always think of Callie as one of the Blume girls, and that was fine. Although she signed legal documents as Calliope Taylor now, she hadn't really considered herself a married woman for almost two years. Not since the day Ethan had abandoned her—and their marriage.

As she often did when she thought about her husband, Callie ran her thumb over the back of her wedding band. These days, she wore the ring mostly for convenience. If she didn't have an irresistibly cute, diaper-clad reason to shy away from legal proceedings, Callie would mail the band to Ethan, divorce him and reclaim her maiden name.

But she didn't want to rekindle her husband's interest in her life. He didn't know about the baby. Thanks to a miracle of science, he had actually left before Callie was pregnant.

A spiraling complexity of fertility treatments had failed during the previous twenty-six cycles, so Callie had held little hope for that last set of appointments at the clinic. And, after all, her husband had left her six weeks before.

She had imagined how wonderful life would be if Ethan came home to such happy news, and she'd kept up with every shot and blood test and ultrasound. Miraculously, the procedure had worked—but Ethan had never returned.

Callie hadn't been able to surrender her broken heart to seek him out and tell him. She'd been alone when she made the decision to try one last time. She'd been alone when she nurtured herself through pregnancy and childbirth. She'd gone on with her life. The eleven-month-old boy was hers alone.

Welcome to the first book in Laura Marie Altom's
U.S. MARSHALS miniseries. There are
four siblings in the Logue family—and they've all
become marshals. Gillian is the only girl, however,
and she sometimes wonders whether
she's cut out for the job, or whether she should
be the traditional woman she thinks
her brothers want her to be. This story takes
place on a small island off the coast of Oregon—
and with Laura's wonderful descriptions,
you can almost smell the ocean!

Available October 2005

"Mr. Morgan?" Gillian Logue called above the driving rain.

The man she sought just stood there at the grumbling surf's edge, staring at an angry North Pacific, his expression far more treacherous than any storm. Hands tucked deep in his pockets, broad shoulders braced against the wind, he didn't even look real—more like some mythical sea king surveying all that was rightfully his.

What had him so deep in thought that he hadn't noticed Gillian approach? Two years had passed since his wife's death. Surely by now he'd let his anger go?

Gillian shivered, hunching deeper into her pathetic excuse for a jacket. Even in the rain, the place reeked of fish and seaweed, and all things foreign to her L.A. beat. They were achingly familiar smells, and she could try all she liked to pretend they didn't dredge up matters best left in the past, but there was no denying it—she had issues with coming home to Oregon. Not that this island was home, but the boulder-strewn coastal landscape sure was.

The crashing waves.

The tangy scent of pines flavored with a rich stew of all things living and dead in the sea.

The times she'd played along the shore as a child.

The times she'd cried along the shore as a woman.

Shoot, who was she to judge Joe?

She wasn't on this godforsaken rock to make a new friend. She was here for one simple reason—to do her job. "Mr. Morgan?" she called again.

He shot a look over his shoulder and narrowed his eyes, not bothering to shield them from the rain. "Yeah," he finally shouted. "That's me. Who are you? What do you want?"

The stiff breeze whipped strands of her blondish hair around her face and she took a second to brush them away before stepping close enough to hold out her hand. "Hi," she said. "I'm U.S. Marshal Gillian Logue." Flipping open a black leather wallet, she flashed him her silver star.

"I asked you a question," he said.

"I heard you." She lifted her chin a fraction higher, hoping the slight movement conveyed at least a dozen messages, the loudest of which was that she might be housed in a small, pretty package, but she considered herself tough as any man—especially him. "I'm here on official business. Over a year ago, the drug lord responsible for killing your wife was released on a technicality. Now we have him back and we'd like you to testify."

The man she'd studied quite literally for months eyed her long and hard, delivered a lifeless laugh of his own then turned his back on her and headed down the beach for the trail leading to his cabin.

"Like it or not, Mr. Morgan, I'm staying!"

Roz Denny Fox, who also writes for Superromance
and Harlequin's new Signature imprint,
is known for the warmth and realness
of her characters and the charm of her writing.
Her first American Romance, TOO MANY BROTHERS,
was published last year, and now we're
delighted to present THE SECRET WEDDING DRESS.
It, too, is an IN THE FAMILY story. Roz strongly
believes in the importance of family and
community, which is reflected in both of
these books. So is her irrepressible sense of humor.
You'll smile and laugh when you read this book—
and you'll feel good.

Available October 2005

Through an open window in her sewing room, Sylvie Shea heard car doors slamming, followed by men's voices, and very briefly, the voice of a child. She was seated on the floor, busily stitching a final row of seed pearls around the hem of an ivory satin wedding dress, but the commotion outside enticed her to abandon her project. Her rustic log cabin nestled into the base of the Great Smoky Mountains didn't exactly sit on a high-volume traffic street—nor did any street in her sleepy hamlet of Briarwood, North Carolina. But as her family reminded her often enough, a woman living alone on the fringe of a forest couldn't be too careful. She'd better spare a moment to investigate.

Pushing aside the dress form that held the cream-colored gown, she squeezed her way through six other forms displaying finished bridesmaids' dresses for her good friend Kay Waller's upcoming nuptials.

A tenth headless mannequin stood in a corner. Sylvie automatically straightened the opaque sheet covering *that* dress, making sure the gown remained hidden from prying eyes. Satisfied the cover was secure, she walked to the oversize picture window she'd had installed in what once served as Bill and Mary Shea's sunporch.

The shouts hadn't abated, and Sylvie parted the curtain she'd sewn from mantilla lace. The filmy weave gave her plenty of light to sew, yet didn't fade any of the fine fabrics stored on bolts along a side wall. Removing the lace filter, a bright shaft of July sun momentarily blinded her.

Blinking several times, at first she couldn't see any reason for the racket. Then as she pressed her nose flat to the sun-kissed glass, Sylvie noticed a large moving van parked in the lane next door.

Iva Whitaker's home had been closed up over a year. At times, Sylvie all but forgot there was a structure beyond her wild-rose covered fence. Iva's land shared a border with Sylvie's, and included a lake fed by a stream running through Sylvie's wooded lot. She often wondered why, when both the Whitakers and the Sheas had owned five acres, they'd built their homes within spitting distance of each other. Iva, though, had been a dear neighbor. If Sylvie was to have new ones, as the moving truck would indicate, she hoped the same could be said of them.

After a moment, she saw a man with straight, honey-blond hair appear, unloading a small pet carrier from a dusty white, seven-passenger van parked to the right of the moving van. He looked thirtyish, was about medium height and had a wiry build. His only real distinguishing feature was gold, wire-rimmed glasses. Sylvie saw him as sort of a corporate version of country singer Keith Urban.

The man set out several suitcases, slammed the hatch and disappeared behind a thicket of colorful sweet peas. Sylvie was left searching her memory bank for particulars of Iva's will. If she'd heard anything said about relatives, she'd forgotten the specifics.

Sylvie made a point of avoiding gossip, the occupational pastime of too many in Briarwood. Five years ago *she'd* been the prime topic. Sylvie doubted a soul among the town's 3,090 residents gave a second thought to how badly the rumors had hurt. Certainly everyone in town was well aware that becoming a top New York City wedding gown designer had been Sylvie's lifelong dream. Her best friends and their parents were privy to the fact she imagined prospective brides coveting a Sylvie Shea gown with the same reverence the rich and famous spoke the name of Vera Wang.

So it'd shocked her that people whispered about her— when at twenty-one, she abruptly left New York and returned home to live in the hand-hewn structure she'd inherited from her father's parents. They must have seen her distress over murmurs claiming she'd left Briarwood at eighteen with stars in her eyes and magic in her fingers, only to return at twenty-one with teary eyes and a heart in tatters.

Broken by a man. Or so gossips speculated then and now. What really happened in New York would remain her humiliating secret.

Come back to Whistler's Bend, Montana, in this
second book of Dianne Castell's humorous
miniseries FORTY & FABULOUS.
Dr. Barbara Jean Fairmont and Colonel Flynn
MacIntire have never gotten along,
but now she needs a favor from him.
B.J. wants a baby, but the trouble is, she's forty,
and husbandless, and qualifying for adoption
is tough. She has an idea for a perfect
arrangement...or does she?

Available October 2005

Dr. Barbara Jean Fairmont peered across the Cut Loose Saloon to Colonel Flynn MacIntire, the guy who'd ran her panties up the high school flagpole, read her diary over the loudspeaker and called her Brainiac. Even if that had happened twenty-two years ago, some things a woman never forgot.

Of course, she also couldn't forget the oatmeal she'd put in his football helmet or her article about jocks running up and down the field because they were lost.

Fairmont and MacIntire, the Brain and the Brawn. They had nothing in common and managed to avoid each other…until now. He was on leave from the army with an injured leg and his grandmother had asked B.J. to help him. He hadn't taken her calls, so tracking him to the saloon was a last-ditch effort.

A country-and-western singer warbled from the jukebox as B.J. snaked her way through sparsely populated tables and a lung-clogging haze of smoke. Flynn sat alone, cigarette in hand, table littered with longnecks, not doing himself one bit of good. "If you quit swilling beer and puffing cancer sticks, agree to get off your butt and do therapy, maybe I can help you."

He looked up, and she gave his two-day beard, wrinkled clothes and incredible ocean-blue eyes a once-over and shuddered. Because of his appearance or because of those eyes?

Unfortunately, because of his eyes…and broad shoulders, and muscled arms and all the other delicious body parts that had driven her secretly insane for as long as she could remember. Usually, her irrational attraction to the man wasn't a problem because Flynn was not around for her to obsess over. But, oh Lordy, he was here now and likely to stay unless he got better and went back to his army life.

He leaned back and folded his arms across his solid broad chest. His index finger on his left hand was slightly crooked, as if it had been broken and not set properly; he had a thick scar on his neck, a wider new one on his chin line, and he was graying at the temples. A soldier. A *fighting* soldier, who'd seen more than his share of combat. She could only imagine what he'd been through and she hated it. But he'd returned alive, and that was something to be hugely thankful for, *though she wished he'd returned somewhere else.*

AMERICAN *Romance*

A three-book series by
Kaitlyn Rice

Heartland Sisters

To the folks in Augusta, Kansas, the three sisters are
the Blume girls—a little pitiable, a bit mysterious and
different enough to be feared.

THE LATE BLOOMER'S BABY
(Callie's story)

Callie's infertility treatments paid off more than a year
after she and her husband split up. Now she's racked
by guilt. She's led her ex-husband to believe the toddler
she's caring for is her nephew, not Ethan's son!

Available October 2005

Also look for:
The Runaway Bridesmaid (Isabel's story)
Available February 2006

The Third Daughter's Wish (Josie's story)
Available June 2006

American Romance
Heart, Home and Happiness

Available wherever Harlequin books are sold.

If you enjoyed what you just read,
then we've got an offer you can't resist!

Take 2 bestselling
love stories FREE!

Plus get a FREE surprise gift!

Clip this page and mail it to Harlequin Reader Service®

IN U.S.A.	IN CANADA
3010 Walden Ave.	P.O. Box 609
P.O. Box 1867	Fort Erie, Ontario
Buffalo, N.Y. 14240-1867	L2A 5X3

YES! Please send me 2 free Harlequin American Romance® novels and my free surprise gift. After receiving them, if I don't wish to receive anymore, I can return the shipping statement marked cancel. If I don't cancel, I will receive 4 brand-new novels every month, before they're available in stores! In the U.S.A., bill me at the bargain price of $4.24 plus 25¢ shipping & handling per book and applicable sales tax, if any*. In Canada, bill me at the bargain price of $4.99 plus 25¢ shipping & handling per book and applicable taxes**. That's the complete price and a savings of at least 10% off the cover prices—what a great deal! I understand that accepting the 2 free books and gift places me under no obligation ever to buy any books. I can always return a shipment and cancel at any time. Even if I never buy another book from Harlequin, the 2 free books and gift are mine to keep forever.

154 HDN DZ7S
354 HDN DZ7T

Name	(PLEASE PRINT)	
Address		Apt.#
City	State/Prov.	Zip/Postal Code

Not valid to current Harlequin American Romance® subscribers.

**Want to try two free books from another series?
Call 1-800-873-8635 or visit www.morefreebooks.com.**

* Terms and prices subject to change without notice. Sales tax applicable in N.Y.
** Canadian residents will be charged applicable provincial taxes and GST.
   All orders subject to approval. Offer limited to one per household.
   ® are registered trademarks owned and used by the trademark owner and or its licensee.

AMER04R   ©2004 Harlequin Enterprises Limited

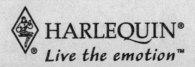

HARLEQUIN *Super***ROMANCE**

**Home to Loveless County...
because Texas is where the heart is.**

**Introducing an exciting new five-book series set in
the rugged Hill Country of Texas.**

Desperate times call for desperate measures. That's why
the dying town of Homestead, Texas, established the
Home Free program, offering land grants in exchange
for the much-needed professional services modern
homesteaders bring with them.

Starting in October 2005 with

BACK IN TEXAS
by Roxanne Rustand
(Harlequin Superromance #1302)

WATCH FOR:

AS BIG AS TEXAS
K.N. Casper (#1308, on sale November 2005)

ALL ROADS LEAD TO TEXAS
Linda Warren (#1314, on sale December 2005)

MORE TO TEXAS THAN COWBOYS
Roz Denny Fox (#1320, on sale January 2006)

THE PRODIGAL TEXAN
Lynnette Kent (#1326, on sale February 2006)

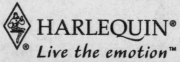

HARLEQUIN®
Live the emotion™

HARLEQUIN®

AMERICAN *Romance*®

The bigger the family, the greater the love—and the more people trying to ruin your life!

THE SECRET WEDDING DRESS
by Roz Denny Fox
(#1087, October 2005)

Betrayed by the man she loved, Sylvie Shea abandoned her career as a wedding dress designer and moved back to her hometown of Briarwood, North Carolina. She's kept only one wedding dress, which nobody's ever seen. The dress she'd planned to wear to her own wedding... Now her delightful but meddling family worries constantly about the lack of romance in Sylvie's life—until Joel Mercer moves next door with his lonely little girl.

Available wherever Harlequin books are sold.